MW00932158

DÉJÀ VIEW

To Amy
Enjoy!
Andrea Burdick

DÉJÀ VIEW

Andrea Shushan Burdick, LICSW

Writers Club Press
New York Lincoln Shanghai

Déjà View

All Rights Reserved © 2003 by Andrea Ilene Burdick

No part of this book may be reproduced or transmitted in any form or by any means, graphic, electronic, or mechanical, including photocopying, recording, taping, or by any information storage retrieval system, without the written permission of the publisher.

Writers Club Press
an imprint of iUniverse, Inc.

For information address:
iUniverse, Inc.
2021 Pine Lake Road, Suite 100
Lincoln, NE 68512
www.iuniverse.com

ISBN: 0-595-26769-6

Printed in the United States of America

For Ed, Rachel and Stacey

Contents

Acknowledgments

I wish to thank the following people whose help was instrumental in creating this book:

First and Foremost—Carroll Smith Sandel, LICSW

The members of my writing groups: Joyce Charter, Shirley Henderson, Louise Gandolfi, Roseanne Curtis, Lori Joyal, Cameron Martin, Nira Porciello, and Linda Gordon. Dr. Venise Berry, PhD. and my fellow writers at the Iowa Summer Writing Festival: Robyn Stevens, Sandie Roberts, Beverly Johnson, Carleen Brice, Sara Smith, Linda and Nicole Rouse, Woody Wallace, Mike McGuire, Linda Rouse, Carol Wright, and Gloria Bond Clunie. A special thank you to fellow clinicians who gave their input or contributed clinical concepts, including Marlene Decker, MFCC, Carol Mc Coin, LICSW, Dr. Maryrose Coiner, PhD., Dr. Hillary Curtis, PhD., Hadley Fisk, LICSW, Jack Hagenbuch, LICSW, Pat Moran, LICSW, and Craig Masten, LICSW. I would also like to extend my appreciation to my friends, Roz Martin, Debra Kaufman and Beth Zagoren who contributed both friendly support and helpful suggestions. I also wish to thank the Marlborough Police Department, especially Lt. Detective Arthur Brodeur.

CHAPTER 1

Diana Lucas

*I*t was happening again. *Why can't I just shut it off? I can't stand seeing it any more!* Diana Lucas sat in the therapist's waiting room listening to the sound of electronically manufactured ocean waves. *Like that's really going to calm somebody down.* Still, she tried to focus on the sound and to clear her mind to meditate, but she was immediately pulled back to the familiar scene in the vision. *What does it mean? Why dead kids?* Diana was startled when the door opened and Zoe introduced herself and gestured for her to come inside the office. Diana sat down, taking in the colorful pictures on the office walls. She chose to sit on the far end of the comfortable beige couch and avoided eye contact with Zoe. She perused the diplomas, licenses and certificates on the wall with a mixture of reverential awe and awkward reticence. "Zoe Leventhal Wentworth, Clinical Social Worker."

Diana anxiously looked at Zoe as if awaiting sentencing while her thoughts continued racing. *She's blond and pretty. I didn't expect that. I bet she is going to think I'm crazy when I tell her about the dream. What kind of sicko dreams about dead kids? What in the hell is the matter with me, anyway? Why isn't she saying anything? Isn't she supposed to be saying something? I hope to God she doesn't expect me to lie down on this couch!* Diana smoothed her navy blue linen suit and reassured Zoe that the directions were excellent and that she had found the office easily. She had dressed carefully that morning so that the therapist would be able to see that she had good self-esteem. Zoe's casual black slacks and short-sleeved tan blouse were accented by a scarf, which was held in place with a simple silver pin. It looked sophisticated and arty, a look which Diana had attempted, but had never quite achieved to her own satisfaction.

"So what brings you here to see me today?" Zoe asked.

"Well, it's kinda hard to talk about, you know, to someone you don't even know or anything…"

"Hmmm." Zoe cooed. "Just take your time."

"It's almost kind of crazy or something." Diana tried to read Zoe's reaction from the expression on her face.

"Crazy?" Zoe smiled pleasantly. Diana felt puzzled and alarmed as she rearranged herself on the couch. This was getting off to a bad start and she started to feel that familiar sensation of drowning and feeling hot at the same time.

"I mean, no, no, not crazy," Diana said, sitting up straighter. "I mean it's not like I'm really crazy or anything. It's not like one of those scenes from *One Flew Over the Cuckoo's Nest* or *What About Bob?* I mean, at least not yet." Diana didn't quite pull off her half-hearted attempt at a smile, but instead heard herself laughing in a high-pitched voice she barely recognized as her own. Diana began examining the plaster on the ceiling and the pattern of swirls as they caught the light. She lowered her gaze to her lap, picked a piece of lint off her tailored blazer, pushed her glasses up her straight slim nose, and then smoothed her long, wavy brown hair. She shot the therapist a brief glance and then quickly averted her eyes again. She gulped before she continued. "Wow! That's a really big eagle on your diploma, there. I never saw such a big diploma. Where did you get that?"

"Boston College."

"That's one big bird!"

Zoe laughed. "One of my other clients actually nicknamed him Big Bird. I hope you don't mind his joining us. He's a very good listener and he hasn't broken a confidence yet." Diana barely noticed Zoe's smile.

"This is harder than I thought it would be. I mean you do this for a living and everything and so you've probably heard all kinds of crazy things from people. But for me, it's my life, and everything, and it's just becoming weirder than I ever thought it could get." Diana paused to check the backs of her earrings to make sure they were still there. Zoe waited patiently, studying Diana, as she resumed her story.

"I see these strange things and sometimes I have this weird kind of feeling that something awful's going to happen."

Zoe waited a while. "So you're feeling troubled by some things that you've been seeing that seem strange to you?" Diana exhaled, relieved that Zoe sounded so matter of fact about it.

"Yeah, it's sometimes in a dream, and sometimes it's in a day dream kind of dream like you get when your mind is wandering. It's been happening all my life."

"Help me to understand. You say this has happened all of your life. So what prompts you to seek help right now? Why now in particular?"

"Well, I'm not sure that I need help, really. I mean it's nice to have help and I'm sure you could help me, but I wouldn't go as far as to say I NEED help or anything. I mean it wasn't even frightening before just recently. It all just seemed so natural back then."

"Back then?" Zoe raised one eyebrow as Diana leaned down to readjust the buckle on her shoes.

"Back when I was a kid, I mean. That's when it started, but for some reason I just accepted it back then. My mother used to tell me I had an overactive imagination if I ever worried about it, and I hardly ever did worry about it as a kid. You know how kids don't ever really worry about anything because they're just too busy playing and pretending?" Diana noticed that Zoe smiled slightly when she said this, but she said nothing, so Diana decided to launch into her story again. "And maybe my mother was right. That's probably just all it is." Diana looked hopefully up at Zoe, lowered her head, stared at the mauve carpeting and then continued, "But no, this is like more than imagination and it's starting to scare me a little. Sometimes I space out so much that even when I'm there it's like I'm not there. I'm probably scaring you right now just talking about it." Diana laughed nervously.

"Oh, I don't scare so easily." Zoe smiled reassuringly.

I wonder if she thinks I'm nuts. "Well, you're probably used to all kinds of fruitcakes and nut cases. But I'm a normal person and that's why this has been so strange. I'm not used to being this far gone. Not to say that I'm far gone, or anything. I mean, I've been wondering if I'm going crazy, and so that's why I'm here, so you can kind of give me a clean bill of mental health and then tell me it's just an overactive imagination." Diana looked down at the nubby fabric on the sofa, rubbing it as she talked. She was working hard at composing herself, but she felt a wild gripping in her chest.

"It sounds like these experiences have really been feeling scary to you." Zoe responded as much to Diana's facial expression and demeanor as she did to her words.

Diana nodded without looking up, and said, "The daydreams are what's scaring me."

"Hmmmm. Tell me about them."

"See, the scary part is not that these daydreams are about such awful Stephen King horror movie kind of things. I mean it's not like Jack Nicholson in *The Shining* is suddenly there with that hideous smile. It's more like just everyday regular stuff. But then the weird part is like when it begins to happen. You asked why I came to see you now, but I don't know, really, I just don't know…"

"When what begins to happen?" Zoe said softly.

Diana hesitated, then looked beseechingly into Zoe's blue eyes. "This is so hard to talk about…"

"I know," Zoe said. "It is hard and I can hear that you're really working hard to help me understand."

"O.K., like, let's say that I picture this little dog inside of a blue car and it's barking because it has been left in the car. O.K., so there's nothing so strange about that and it's not like the dog had fangs or rabies with foam coming out of his mouth, or anything. But then, let's say I go to the store and I look at the car next to me and there it is. It's the same car and it's the same dog. Only this time it's not a day dream and this time it really is there." Diana's hand began trembling slightly as she continued to rub the upholstery fabric. "You, know? It was a dream before and now it's real? Everyone always says they want their dreams to come true, but they wouldn't if they knew what it was like when they do come true."

"Hmmmm. What's that like for you?"

"It's like pretending getting mixed up with reality. You know?" Diana took off her glasses and audibly sighed to fog up each lens before polishing it with a tissue.

Zoe noticed that Diana's lower lip was quivering. "And I can see that this is really troubling you."

"Yeah, well, you know, the big joke is whenever I tell my friends about this they say it's just déjà vu all over again, like Yogi Berra said, and I should stop worrying about it. You don't think I really am going crazy do you? I mean in your professional opinion and everything?"

"Well, I can tell you that I've worked with a lot of crazy people over the years and they've told me a lot of crazy things. But the people who ask me if they're going crazy aren't usually the ones who are crazy. Crazy people usually have no idea that what they say and do is crazy. That's what makes them crazy." Diana relaxed visibly, and exhaled as Zoe continued. "I do think we'll need some time to discover what's been confusing and upsetting to you about what you've been experiencing. It certainly seems like you've been taking a sensible approach in sorting this out with me here today."

Diana looked out the window at the trees reflecting on Hager Pond. Impossible hues of gold, red, maroon, yellow and orange were just beginning to paint the predominantly green leaves of September with the colors of Fall. It was so much more beautiful than the pond in the dream. "And you haven't even heard the freaky part yet," she said to Zoe. "Do you want to hear the strangest part? It's a dream. Do you do dreams?" Zoe nodded a welcoming, and Diana continued. "I had this dream about some dead kids in a pond. This one was like a regular dream-dream and not a daydream. Anyway, in the dream, dead kids were being pulled out of a pond by cops or firemen or something. It was a dark, scummy pond that was all full of this marshy glop. And creepy trees were hanging down, those furry, hairy kind of trees, all mossy like. And I didn't know where it was or anything, or who these kids were. And there were these long hanging vines. It was sort of like a cross between a swamp scene and a Tarzan movie kind of jungle thing, but not really. Anyway, there were a bunch of cops there and this pitiful little cabin near the pond, all ramshackle and broken down. I could just picture it, like I was seeing it in my mind's eye. Like a movie, or more like a video where you can freeze frame it on different scenes. They looked so white and clammy, kind of waxy like."

Zoe's face mirrored Diana's grimacing.

"And I always dream in color and that just makes it worse, doesn't it? All their veins were all blue and right at the surface or more like almost purplely. It was really horrible." Diana lowered her head and covered her face with her hands.

"It does sound ghastly," Zoe soothed. Diana picked up her head and looked at Zoe hopefully.

"Well, it was. But you know that dreams are weird, and so you kind of expect that. But then the really strangest part was later on. Look at my arm! I'm getting goose bumps just thinking about it!

Anyway, I was watching *CNN Headline News* while I walked on my treadmill. I like to get my exercise every day. That's the great thing about *CNN Headline News*. You just keep going 'til you get back around to the same part of the news again, and no matter when you start you'll get your half an hour of exercise. Anyway, there I am exercising, watching TV, and they show this scene from somewhere in Arkansas or Alabama or something. It was one of those 'A' states. And it was there, like the dream in the pond. Everything the same…the cops…the cabin. And they said that this man had murdered all of his seven children and thrown their bodies in the pond. I just wigged out. I've never even been to Arkansas or Atlanta or wherever, but it sure looked just like the scene from my dream. They were pulling out all of these different size kid bodies and putting them in these zipper-up body bag kind of things. They were really showing the whole thing, only it was from far away so you couldn't tell on TV how pale they were and everything. They didn't show them up close like I saw them in my dream. But it was just like you said, ghastly. That's a really good word for it, because it WAS ghastly. Anyhow, I had this dream two weeks ago and they were just running the story last week, and they said it just happened that day. And you know what that means…"

"What does that mean?" Zoe asked, raising both eyebrows.

"It means that I dreamed this before it happened in real life, and that is just too bizarre. Now you can see why I really couldn't explain it all that well when we talked on the phone."

"Hmmmm."

"At first I tried to tell myself it was just a coincidence. A 'co-inky-dink' as my mother used to call it. It's not like they have some news report on exactly seven dead kids being pulled from a pond every day, is it? I never heard a story like that before, have you?"

Zoe admitted that she hadn't.

Diana felt shaky. *Oh, God, I'm not going to start crying now, am I?* "That's when I called to make the appointment with you, only I didn't know then that it was going to be you, of course. But when I ever saw 'Hager Pond Counseling Associates' in the phone book, I just knew I should come here, because of the pond in the dream and the pond in the name of this place. Kind of like a sign, you know? But dreaming things before they even happen in real life. Is that not strange, or what?" Diana sighed heavily and leaned back on the couch.

"How do you explain that to yourself?" Zoe asked.

"Well, that's just the thing. I keep trying to explain it to myself, and it's just not very explainable, is it? Now I'm scared like what if my dreaming it made it happen or something? Like what if this is proof I have powers? Don't worry. I'm not nutty enough to really think I have powers, but you know? Sometimes I think I do have powers. I was hoping you could explain it to me, because it has me so tense that I'm a bundle of nerves wrapped up with tension wire. I've been such a nervous wreck since that dream you called ghastly, or, no, really it was since the news report. So anyway, that's what I was thinking about at three o'clock in the morning when I couldn't sleep. It's worse these days with digital clocks, isn't it? You know you woke up at exactly three-twenty-three or whatever, and you just see these glowing red numbers staring back at you. But anyway, while I'm lying there and I can't fall back to sleep, I'm thinking 'I have to see somebody to help me.' Actually, the word ghastly is almost an under-statement, now that I think about it."

"O.K. Help me out, here. I'm still a bit confused. You say you have been having these experiences all your life, and yet they have just recently begun to frighten you. Am I right so far?"

"Yep."

"So what's different about now?" Zoe noted that Diana had been escalating the pace of her speech as she went on.

Diana felt like she was talking and holding her breath at the same time. She took a moment to catch her breath and then she contin-ued. "Now I have proof, see? Proof of my powers. I don't know why it's scaring me so much more now, except for that thing on CNN. I didn't want my visions to become famous, or anything. And once something is on CNN, it's famous whether you want it to be or not."

Zoe nodded and returned a calming, "Hmmmm."

Diana gulped, feeling her Adam's apple bulging in her throat. "And I can hardly remember not having them, they've been with me so long. They started when I was really little, like three or four. That's what therapists want people to talk about, isn't it, about their childhood? People say you can't remember back that far but I can. My grandmother used to rock me in her big rocking chair when I was a little girl, whenever I got the visions. That's what she called them, back then, 'the visions,' and she told me she had been getting them all of her life too. Do you think it could be hereditary or something? I used to like it because it made me feel special and kind of like my little secret with Grandma that was just ours. I loved sitting on her lap like that. Parents are always busy, you know? But grandparents have time because they aren't going anywhere. I used to sit on Grandma's lap, sucking my thumb. I was always sucking my thumb when I was a kid. Probably a sign of insecurity, right?"

Zoe smiled and nodded.

"I read a lot so I know these things. That's why I liked the visions back then, because of Grandma and…then after she was gone. But now I can't think straight. I have to be able to concentrate to do my work without my powers getting in the way. It's hard for me to stay on the phone at work, because I can't get anything done when I just keep seeing it over and over in my mind's eye. I work as a recruiter at an employment agency. My friends always say it's the perfect job for me because I get to talk on the phone all day. I love to talk, but you probably noticed that already. So anyway, my best friend Roz at the office says, 'A headhunter going to see a headshrinker?' Pretty funny, huh?"

Zoe smiled and Diana felt riveted to her clear blue eyes. "So, anyway, I'm on the phone all day and I have to keep track of a lot of details. And I've tried to keep good notes. Like my friend Roz always says, 'Plan your work and work your plan.' Only now, when I try to work my plan, I'm just going over it and over it…you know?" Diana stopped there to take in a long breath. She shook her head slowly and looked down again. "I haven't had a placement in two months, It's…" Diana started, but gave up again. She looked at Zoe pleadingly. "I'm used to being successful. I'm the top biller in the office. I'm…" Diana gave up again, but this time Zoe prompted her.

"You're concerned that it's starting to impact your functioning at work, and it didn't before?"

Diana felt a brief flash of anger. *Just how nutty does she think I am, anyway? Now I've got her thinking that I can't even function.* "Well, yeah, but I only look like a basket case, on the outside, but really I'm not. But it's just that it keeps interrupting me with worrying about it. I will be right in the middle of thinking about something I have to do but then that creepy feeling comes back where you have a knot in your stomach and butterflies along with the knot and they are all grinding up together in there. Anyway, it just feels nasty, and you're trying to swallow this big lump in your throat that doesn't want to go down. Sorry that was so gross. I hope you don't mind gross stuff. Does any of this make sense? It's not like I'm some loser, or anything. It's amazing that I'm doing as well as I am, considering how weird and ghastly this all is. I'm always surprised at how well I'm doing. And doing well in ghastly circumstances is even better. I guess that's the answer to the question you asked! The real reason that I'm here now is that I'm suddenly doing so much better than I've ever done before." Diana sat back and heaved a gasping sigh.

"So you've come for help right now because you're suddenly doing so much better?" Zoe asked doubtfully.

Diana felt stricken. "That doesn't make any sense, does it? But really, maybe it is interfering with my life, because, I mean, why would I be here if it wasn't? When you have trouble eating because there's that big gross lump in your throat, and you're sleeping with your worst nightmares, and floating instead of concentrating, well, yeah, I guess you could say it's impacting my functioning if you wanted to." Diana ripped a facial tissue out of the box in front of her and began twisting it. "It's been going on all my life, but I kept pretending it wasn't. Once you see seven dead kids right on *CNN Headline News* you can't tell yourself it's just 'déjà vu' anymore. What if the visions have all happened somewhere else and I just didn't know it? Or what if my dreams make things happen? I know that sounds really crazy, but it is possible. I don't want to keep seeing hideous scenes like a bunch of instant replays in my head. I feel like I'm not real sometimes, like I'm just floating around outside of my body. I just want to be normal, and seeing news stories in your head all day before they even happen in real life is just not normal."

"As non-stop as *CNN Headline News*," Zoe mused.

"Yeah, only this time I want the treadmill to stop, you know?"

CHAPTER 2

Zoe & Daniel Wentworth

Zoe Wentworth quickly pecked in her home phone number as soon as Diana Lucas left. As usual, she had planned the timing to be as close as a quarter inch seam. *C'mon, Daniel, Pick up the phone.*

"Hello?"

"Daniel, good, it's you. How are things going back at the ranch?"

"No problems here. We called out for pizza, so we've eaten, the girls are doing homework, and we're good to go. I got a chicken sandwich for you to eat in the car on the way. I'll be right over to get you."

"Thanks, honey. Could you bring me a Diet Coke too? They're in the fridge."

"I think that could be arranged."

"That's great! I don't think anything makes me feel more power-less than having my car in the shop. Thanks for making it as painless as possible." Zoe picked up her tote bag and filled it with paperwork she would have to do later that night after the Open House at the kids' school. As she came down the stairs she created the same famil-iar creaks in all of the usual spots that had become a kind of musical fanfare when someone descended the staircase, wordlessly announc-ing the end of each session of words. She noticed the computer at the front desk and thought of how incongruous it looked in the antique surroundings. She looked out the ancient wavy window glass and she could barely see the flying goose weather vane on the top of the gazebo just on the other side of the parking lot. *This 350 year old house is a place where I hear so many stories, and I bet it could tell stories of its own. The window glass has sat for so many years in its tiny panes that it is reverting to its original liquid form. By now, no one even remembers that the reason the panes were cut into little pieces was to avoid paying taxes on larger sheets of glass. And so it is with my clients, and with me, too sometimes. We move in patterns and see through distortions based on the past, without remembering why we did what we did, or why we're still doing it.*

Zoe waited only briefly before Daniel drove up. He was tall, slim and had dark brown hair that was starting to grey at the temples, and diminish at the top, in a circle, like a monk. He had a full beard and moustache since he got his hair trimmed as infrequently as possible. He and Zoe had met when they were students at the University of California at Berkeley as undergraduates. Zoe slid in, fastened her seatbelt, stashed her belongings, popped open the can of soda and placed it in the beverage holder, carefully unwrapped her sandwich and began eating it while Daniel was still methodically readjusting the mirrors. Soon they were moving down the narrow, meandering country roads, as Zoe marveled again at the quaint New England landscape. After living in Marlborough, Massachusetts for twelve years, she had come to love the stone walls, the split log fences, and the trunks of white birches silhouetted against the red and orange leaves that emblazoned the woods every autumn.

"No matter how long we live here, I still can't get over how beautiful it is, especially during Fall color season. Remember when we first came out here from California when you had the interview with Digital? I remember thinking how it all seemed like the phony façade of a movie set. What else would an L.A. lady think? I half expected to turn the corner and see that it was all only three inches thick and only there for the camera. It seemed too good to be true. I never thought we could own a home like ours. I remember going around with the realtor, looking at these gorgeous colonial homes with shingles on the windows, four and five bedrooms, two and three bathrooms, on wooded property with more than an acre of land, and thinking we'd died and gone to house hunter's heaven. That's back when the prices here were so low in comparison to California. We'd never have been able to get a house like that at home."

"I don't think there are any homes like that in California," Daniel said.

"You know what I mean. An equivalent California style house. I remember I kept expecting the real estate agent to show us the guest cottage because I could never believe that the house was actually in our price range."

"In California a large cracker box was out of our price range."

"That's what I mean. We're lucky, and I never take that for granted." Zoe carefully picked two pieces of shredded lettuce off of her blouse, checking to make sure that no mayonnaise had accompanied them.

"I know. I look around sometimes and I feel the same way. A lot of good things came together at once for us. Don't forget how much I wanted the job here too. I had offers in Silicon Valley, but the one I really wanted was here. And it's turned out to be such a good move. They made me an offer I couldn't refuse. We were very lucky with timing and location," Daniel said.

"We've been lucky with a lot of things, if you want to call it luck. We've made some tough decisions and they've played out well for us, but nothing is perfect. It's been hard for the kids to grow up so far away from their grandparents and I miss my parents a lot, especially at the Jewish holidays. The kids grow up so fast. Who would have ever thought we would wind up on the East Coast? The girls are fourth generation native Californians on your side and no one out here even believes that anyone is a native Californian. We both thought we would live our whole lives there, but that just goes to show you that you just don't know where life will take you. And sometimes it takes us to bigger places than we expected. Remember how Rebecca, who was three at the time of the move, had been reluctant to go upstairs on the day we moved out of the hotel room and into the house? Remember? She asked, 'Who lives up there, Mommy?' Remember when we told her we live in the whole house, both upstairs and downstairs, she started giggling. She thought we were teasing her. I remember those big brown eyes getting wider and how she giggled when she went upstairs and found her toys." *What a fun age that was!*

"Yeah. She just couldn't believe we had all that space, especially after spending three months in a hotel room. I remember driving up to the house at night when we had just moved in she asked me, 'Daddy, why did the moon move here from California when we did?'"

"See that's where we're really lucky. The kids. That's what it's all about. They were so adorable, weren't they? And they still are, but it's hard to remember that sometimes when you're struggling with adolescents who are working so hard to separate by pushing you away. Where did all the years go? Teenagers! Both of them! It's been a long haul, a hasn't it?"

"It's been fun," Dan said, smiling.

Zoe looked at her husband and tried to remember the last time it had felt fun to her. "Remember I was so excited when I got accepted by Boston College social work grad school? I knew it would be a struggle to manage the children and graduate school at the same time, I just didn't realize how much of a struggle! I think that had to be the toughest. Managing my internship, clinical supervision, going to classes, writing papers, doing research projects and trying to hold the house together, however unsuccessfully. I remember I used to feel like I had to say to the girls, 'I'm sorry I don't have time for you. I'm just too busy helping people whose parents didn't have time for them.' And I used to worry that I was putting too much of a burden on you on top of all of the demands of your career. There is always so much to do that it's overwhelming. Jessie said to me once, 'You only realize you're juggling too many balls after you drop one of them.' As hard as that time in graduate school was, that was back when the girls wanted more time with us, before the hormones hit. Lately, they're either on the phone with friends, planning an escape with friends, or out with friends."

"Well, they still seem to want to spend time with me. Rebecca is always asking me to take her out driving and Leah is always wanting me to help her with her math homework and so on. Are you sure you're reading them accurately? You can't take these things personally."

"Maybe it's a mother and daughter thing. Just this morning Rebecca said to me, 'God, Mom, you're not wearing that, are you? That's so twentieth century!' I felt like I was back in high school myself, trying to fit in and be popular. After that, I overheard Leah saying, 'Rebecca, leave Mom alone. She's old and all the old people just don't get it. It doesn't matter anyway, because none of her friends will even notice.' That did little to help me remember not to take it personally."

"Look, you're the grown-up here. Rebecca and Leah are kids, they're not the fashion police. Where is your usual confidence? What's up with you?"

"Well, remember how you told me yesterday about that big bonus that you got at work?"

"Yeah?"

"Well, I guess if I'm really going to own my feelings, I'm jealous. I work really hard in a difficult field that requires so much training, on-going high level clinical thinking, and an emotional component that is rarely a part of people's work. And for this I am so poorly compensated as a social worker that I feel devalued, dismissed and embarrassed. I get no benefits, no holiday pay, no sick pay, no vacation pay, and no pay at all any time anyone decides not to come in. The only reason I am there is that you are subsidizing my being there. I should be happy and grateful that you make enough money that I can do what I really want to do, which is counseling. Instead, I am just so furious that I work so hard in the non-profit sector and get so poorly compensated while you work so hard in the business sector and get so much. And to top it all off, the kids are O.K. with you and I am somehow at the top of their shit list. Meanwhile, I love you, I don't see you doing anything at all wrong, you are a wonderful husband and provider, so on top of being jealous I feel guilty for feeling jealous when I should be happy. Any other questions?"

"Yeah. If you were your own client and you came to you and said all of that what would you tell yourself?"

"I would tell myself that this is all about the healthcare delivery system in twenty-first century America, "fee-for-service" therapy and managed care. It really does suck, and I am neither wholly responsible for how it works nor wholly responsible for fixing it. I would say that given the circumstances that it is only human to feel jealous, because it's a tough situation. I would say that any and all feelings are just feelings and we have no reason to feel guilty about our feelings. We feel what we feel. I would tell myself that we cannot make ourselves feel something we don't just because it is more socially acceptable."

"Well, it sounds to me like you're a hell of a good therapist. Of course, I couldn't give you a professional opinion on that, not being in the field. myself, so what do you think?" Dan asked, as they pulled into the parking lot at the college prep Ashcroft School their daughters attended.

"A lot of times I think I'm a damn good therapist, too, now that you mention it, but sometimes in the absence of positive input from others, I lose my confidence. I try not to measure my success by how much money I make, but if I'm really honest with myself I'd have to say that this culture really does impact how I feel about myself as a professional. It's just a challenge to feel like I'm successful when I make so little money."

"I think a lot of hurting people are damn lucky to have you. And here's what I think about money. Money can be shared."

"And I'm damn lucky to have you too. You actually would have made a good therapist. Did you notice how you served as a catalyst for me to come up with my own answer on that?"

"Me a therapist? Are you kidding? Somebody has to make a living!" Dan smiled broadly as they got out of the cars and walked across the parking lot, and underneath the *Back to School Night* banner that had been strung across the entryway. "So how about if you be Rebecca and I'll be Leah tonight?" he asked as he reached into his shirt pocket and handed Zoe Rebecca's schedule.

"That sounds good to me, especially since Leah has been struggling with her math and you're the one who helps her with it. The timing of this is actually wonderful. After I hear all the teachers telling me what a pleasure it is to have Rebecca in their classes I know I'll be *kvelling* and I'll come home feeling so much better about her. We always hear what a wonderful student she is at these things."

"I like *kvelling* about our kids, too, so this should be fun."

Fun. There's that word again. "Okay, I'll see you after school!" Zoe said, kissing him briefly as they parted company.

CHAPTER 3

Tina Ormond

ina Ormond received particularly beautiful roses from her husband Joe for her birthday, with delicate hues of pale pink and a bolder pink swirled together. There must have been two dozen of them, and they almost melted away the anger she had been feeling towards him. She carefully placed the nearly perfect roses in a large green vase, leaning forward to smell their aroma. The fragrance, which filled the room with sweetness, brought back memories of their early courtship. Joe used to tell her that she was pretty, that her shiny black hair and dark eyes, her tiny frame and her refined features made her look like the 'Princess' he called her. Tina was amazed that such a good-looking man who could get any woman he wanted would be interested in her. Joe had seemed so romantic then, promising to protect her and provide for her all of the things that she expected from family: structure, security and guidance.

Tina believed that Joe really cared about her by the way that he guarded her closely, helped her to understand the ways of the world, and taught her what she needed to know in order to please him. Like her own father, Joe was old-fashioned and sentimental, something Tina still loved about him. He didn't want Tina to work, wanted to take her out shopping in order to help her pick out beautiful clothes, and he hoped to have a close-knit family, just as she did. Joe worked hard, fixing cars in an auto body shop, so that Tina would be able to stay home with their children once they started a family. When Tina found out she was pregnant they were so excited. Tina felt hopeful that she would find the same kind of family connection as a mother that she had enjoyed as a child, loved by a strict, over-protective father and a warm and loving mother. When the baby was born, Joe was ecstatic that it was a little boy, and the couple promptly agreed to name him Joseph Ormond, Jr. The baby had a full head of the same dark, wavy hair that his father had. Joe adored Joey, as they called him, and doted on him, helping Tina with every decision pertaining to his care and up-bringing. Despite Joe's sometimes drinking too much, Tina felt he was a good husband until the harrowing episode at the end of her pregnancy. Joe had been under a tremendous amount of stress at work, had stopped at the bar on the way home, and he was in a miserable mood by the time he came home. Tina had been alone in an empty house all day and she wanted to go out for dinner. When Joe came home to find that his dinner wasn't ready, he lost his temper and he slapped Tina, shoved her, and finally kicked her pregnant belly so hard that he knocked her halfway across the kitchen.

Joe had been shocked and frightened by his own behavior. "I don't know what's wrong with me," he said, sobbing, "what if I hurt the baby?" Joe wanted to take Tina straight to the hospital so that the doctors could reassure him that the baby was all right. He knew it was a boy, based on the ultrasound, and he had already begun calling his son "Little Joey." But he needed to make sure that he wouldn't get into trouble.

"When you get to the hospital, just tell them you fell," Joe said to Tina, and she was so embarrassed that Joe had gotten so drunk that he hit her, that she actually felt relieved at the thought of telling the doctors this little lie. After all, it wasn't as though Joe would ever have touched her if he hadn't been drinking. It wasn't really her Joe who had hurt her, at all. It was really the alcohol. Joe promised not to drink, bought her a beautiful bassinet for the baby, and came home with a new car borrowed from work so that she and the baby could travel home from the hospital in style.

After Tina saw the tears in Joe's eyes as he watched his son emerge in the delivery room, she remembered why she married Joseph Ormond. Joe adored the baby, wanted to hold him, dressed him up in baby Red Sox outfits, and loved showing him off in public. Just after the birth, Tina felt pleased with all of the lavish attention Joe showered on Joey, reassured that the beating late in her pregnancy had only been an aberration. She felt confident that Joe was going to be a good husband and father as soon as he gave up liquor once and for all. Still, she could not shake off her nagging doubts that he would really be able to stop drinking.

Joey was born jaundiced and had to stay in the hospital's newborn nursery a little longer than most infants, so Tina and Joe had the opportunity to go celebrate their new son's arrival with a special evening out at the Wildwood Steak House. Joe had ordered champagne for both of them, and he even kept his promise not to drink too much of it. It was then that Joe had given Tina his grandmother's diamond pendant, which he had inherited. Joe told Tina, "This is to let you know how much I love you and appreciate you for giving me a son."

Tina had never owned anything as dazzling and valuable as that diamond, and it almost erased the empty feelings she had in the recovery room the day that Joey was born. Tina was hurt that Joe said nothing about loving her, rushing off instead to call his mother the moment little Joey was born. When Joe's family came over to the hospital to see her baby, no one seemed to even notice Tina. As soon as everyone left, Tina began crying again. She ached with the loss of her own parents who had died in quick succession less than three years before. She told herself that Joe and Joey were her family now. But where was her big, strong Joe, who always had always promised to take care of her? Joe told her he wanted to go over to his favorite bar so that he could pass out cigars to all of the other guys. Tina didn't try to stop him, even though she wanted to scream, "What about me?" Instead, she pulled the curtain closed around her hospital bed and sobbed quietly into her pillow, trying to muffle the sound so that her roommate wouldn't hear. After all, hadn't the doctor said that the hormonal changes after birth might make her cry? Even now, ever since their romantic evening out, whenever Tina doubted Joe, she looked at the brilliantly sparkling diamond, turning it to catch the light reflecting off of each and every facet. Then she would feel reassured once again that she was cared for. And that even worked, for a while.

CHAPTER 4

Jessica Lakewood

G roup Supervison was hardly a group that day since Zoe and Jessica Lakewood, her close friend and colléague, were the only ones there. Jessica was over six feet tall, with frizzy red hair and a long, triangular face splashed with ginger colored freckles that matched her eyes. Dr. Simon Abrahams, the psychiatrist, was out sick again. He suffered from Obsessive Compulsive Disorder and he spent his life looking for germs that he could kill while convinced that germs were seeking him out to kill him. His daily hand washing rituals left his hands red and raw and his patients met with him in a darkened room lit by a small table lamp and the greenish glow of his phases of the moon calendar. He was convinced that he could predict how his patients would do based on the phases of the moon, and he encouraged everyone else to keep track of lunar influences as he did. Virginia Remington, the Clinical Director, was out on another one of her exotic vacations, trekking through Sri Lanka. Zoe relished the thought of having the luxury of talking with Jessica one on one.

"How are Anna and the baby?" Zoe asked. Anna Lambert was Jessica's lesbian partner and she was out on maternity leave, having given birth to their first child, Bridget. A sperm bank had supplied the father. Zoe and Jessica had been friends since they were in Graduate School together at BC. It was Jessica's turn to present the case today, and she was always one to get right down to business.

"They're fine. Sleepy, but fine. You know how it is with the waking up every few hours all night. But Anna says she is really enjoying her time at home," Jessica said wistfully. "I wish I could spend more time with Bridget too."

"Sounds nice. I loved that time with Rebecca and Leah. I used to just love looking at them and watching their little newborn ways of moving. Tell Anna I said hello, and tell her to enjoy the baby now while she is still too young to talk back."

Jessica smiled broadly as she attempted to imagine the baby talking, let alone talking back. "I will," she promised.

"And how about Stephen? How is he doing?" Zoe asked.

Stephen was Jessica's 17-year-old son from her now defunct marriage. Jessica had begun by thinking she could become a heterosexual if she just tried hard enough. She found out that she was mistaken, but Stephen was a wonderful gift that had come into her life from that failed attempt. She and Charlie, Stephen's father, had somehow managed to remain good friends and to be successful co-parents.

"Stephen's fine, thanks," Jessica said. "He and Charlie just went to visit Charlie's folks in Florida. He's back in school now, but they really had a great time. I'm so glad and lucky that Charlie has stayed in his life. I know the research shows how few men manage to hang in there with their kids after a divorce. And Stephen just adores Charlie. He also loves his grandparents, although they make a few digs now and then about the 'lifestyle your mother chose with Anna.' They make it sound like it's a fashion decision. Should I wear a scarf or a necklace? Should I be a lesbian with Anna or a heterosexual wife with Charlie? But Stephen told me that Charlie just tells them to knock it off and they do, at least in front of him. Stephen seems so well balanced around it, probably because he knows how much both of his parents love him. Or all three of his parents if you count Anna. And I think he does. He's just such a great kid," Jessica said, beaming.

"And Rebecca informs me that she considers him 'a hunk' too. I think they were eyeing each other a bit when you all came over to swim this past August."

Jessica smiled broadly. "Well, I can only applaud Rebecca for her good taste in boys. I think he's pretty adorable myself. And she is so gorgeous with her long brown hair and those big brown eyes. Really, Zoe, she is just beautiful and she has such a perfect figure. No wonder Stephen couldn't keep his eyes off her. Anyway, I guess we should start. I have a new client to present today, and get a load of this. His name is Nestor Pewkes." Jessica leaned back, waiting for Zoe's reaction.

"I hope for his sake that you are kidding. With the last name of Pewkes his family actually named him Nestor? Doesn't that qualify as child abuse?" Zoe said.

"It should."

"Well, I can guess his first problem—going through life with a name like that. Yikes!" Zoe exclaimed.

"That's the least of his problems, believe me. His mother brought him to the first session."

Zoe raised that one eyebrow when she heard this. "How old is he?"

"Mid-thirties," Jessica said.

"Oh my God! She didn't come into the session with him did she?" Zoe asked.

"She wanted to, but naturally I wouldn't allow it. And he came by himself to the second session."

"Progress already," Zoe said, nodding slightly.

"Yeah. He has a really strange presentation. He has such limited language and social skills that it is often hard to keep the session going. He seems to have social phobia and a kind of paralysis of speech. He just stops mid-sentence and looks at me as if he were trying to get me to finish his thoughts for him, blinking away and flaring his nostrils. He literally talks about nothing, and as far as I can tell, he also has nothing going on in his life except Mom, and he doesn't say much about her, either. It's not like he's tied to Mom by her apron springs, it's more like he has her apron strings tied around his neck like a noose."

"Great image. Sounds grim. What enabled him to come in for treatment?" Zoe asked.

"He presented with 'I want to meet girls and Mom wants me to meet girls, too. Mom thought I should get some counseling so I could learn how to talk to girls.'"

"Yeah, I'll just bet Mom wants him to meet girls." Zoe said in her most cynical tones. "So now what are you supposed to be, a dating service?"

"He couldn't tolerate a date, even if he could get one,"

"How is his functioning? Does he work?"

"Yes, he's an accountant. He's high functioning in some ways. Successful at work. Very rigid and fixed, everything just so. He told me at a recent session that his stomach turned when he discovered he made a minor error at work."

"Wow. Anything else that Mom has going on in her life that might be having an impact on him?" Zoe asked, doodling on a piece of paper as they discussed the case.

"What life? Neither one of them has a life outside of each other."

"So what does he talk about while he's talking about nothing?" Zoe asked.

"The weather. His trip to the grocery store. Should he buy a new car or fix the one he has? Where can he find a spare part to fix his car? How relieved he was that he didn't have to buy a new car. How he received a letter that was meant for his neighbor and his reluctance to ring her doorbell to return it. Anxiety about going into a convenience store to buy a newspaper. What would the pretty desk clerk at 7-11 think of him? Could she be the girl he is looking for? His demeanor is very serious, flat affect, no expression, very wooden. And he's very concrete. During the first session, when I gave him my standard opening line of 'What brings you here today?' he actually said, 'My car.'"

Zoe laughed. "Concrete and wooden, huh? So which material best describes what he's made of? Wood or concrete?"

Jessica considered this with that serious expression of hers. "I'd have to say concrete wins out. During the initial assessment I asked him 'What would things look like if they were exactly the way you wanted them to be?' He thought for a while and said, 'What would they look like? Well the house would look clean.' Apparently, Mom can't keep the place tidy enough for Nestor. He talked about how unbearable and nauseating it was to find a hair in the sink—how it turned his stomach."

"Wow! So what are we calling this case? *As The Stomach Turns*, or *Why Nestor Pukes*?" Zoe asked.

Zoe and Jessica laughed uproariously, and Jessica slapped her knee while Zoe laughed so hard she was afraid she would wet her pants. "We're terrible!" Jessica said to Zoe.

"Sometimes ya gotta laugh to keep from crying," Zoe said with smiling eyes that were just beginning to show a trace of crow's feet.

"Hell, if we didn't laugh once in a while how could we deal with this stuff? Remember the day we laughed our asses off discussing the case of that really obese client you had. What was her name again? I remember she had an unusual name."

"India."

"India, yeah, right. You were always worried that she was going to take another overdose. Whatever happened to her, anyway? I haven't heard you talk about her in a long time."

"Believe it or not, she had to terminate because her insurance company cut her off. I still worry about her because she really needs to be in treatment."

"Oh, that's a shame. So any suggestions here, Zoe, besides a cleaning service? I think Simon would vote for that one if he were here." Jessica had already returned to that earnest look of hers.

"Simon wouldn't be Simon if he were here. But anyway, back to your client. Where's Dad?" Zoe asked.

"There never was a dad. Dad was a one night stand when Mom went out on her first date, and Mom got drunk enough that she didn't even remember the next morning how he got her into bed the night before. When she found out she was pregnant she decided to keep the baby. Very Catholic and no birth control, let alone abortions."

"That figures. Does Mom still drink?" Zoe asked.

"Oh, no. She never did, really. She just allowed this guy to succeed in getting her drunk enough that he could take advantage of her, I guess. And she loses no opportunity to tell Nestor the evils of alcohol and how that one night of drinking destroyed her life."

Zoe pondered this. "So she is basically telling him that his birth destroyed her life and that intimate connections are dangerous."

"Yeah. If you can call sex with some guy you barely know intimate," Jessica said, taking a sip of coffee from the large mug she almost always had with her.

"Good point. So where are you going with him?" Zoe asked.

"At the moment he is working on some basic skills like how to talk to another human being. He is so awkward and uncomfortable that it is painful just to sit with him and watch his struggle to say something. He reminds me of a foreign film that someone has forgotten to dub. His mouth opens, but nothing comes out. He just can't talk."

"But you know, for the time you've been seeing him, he has actually told you a lot about himself. You seem to know about his family, Mom's history, and so on," Zoe said. "There is some pertinent content there."

"Yeah, I guess that's true. But it's been like watching a tropical fish in an aquarium, mouth gaping open, and then shut, with no sound emitted. It's so much work just to extract words from him, although he is perhaps a bit more fluent than he was before."

"The treatment seems on track to me, Jessie. You may want to discuss him in supervision with Virginia when she gets back, but it sounds to me like you're right where you need to be with him. And I have no doubt that he's right where he needs to be with you, too. As Rebecca and Leah would say, 'He just needs to get a life.'"

"Thanks for the input, Zoe. Let me know if you think of any other ideas later. Your kids could be right; he does need to get a life—one that's separate from Mom's."

"Oh, you're more than welcome, and keep me informed on how he's doing."

"Speaking of the kids, I was wondering about your holiday plans for this year. Can you believe they already have Christmas decorations out in the stores right next to the Halloween costumes? I think they put them out earlier every year." Jessica took another gulp of her coffee.

"Well, of course you know we're on for Thanksgiving at our house again. That's become our tradition. I hope you and your family can come."

"We wouldn't dream of missing it. As long as you're going to be okay with the baby being there."

"Are you kidding? Of course the baby is welcome to come! Then after Thanksgiving we'll skip our usual Chanukah party because we plan to take the kids out to see my parents in California for Chanukah. Then we'll have our Christmas at home, as usual." Zoe said, smiling warmly at her friend, her eyes crinkling at the corners.

"Zoe, you know I'm confused about something. You talk a lot about being Jewish, but then you celebrate Christmas and Chanukah."

"I celebrate all Hallmark holidays! I just celebrate Christmas the same way I celebrate Halloween, Valentine's Day and St. Patrick's Day. We have fun, and we don't think too much about the original religious connections. Daniel grew up with Christmas and he wanted to continue that tradition with the kids, and I grew up with

Chanukah, always feeling left out at Christmas. So now, I think I make a bigger deal about Christmas than Daniel does. I have a lot of fun decorating the house and the tree. We just do the Santa Claus and jingle bells kind of Christmas rather than a religious Christmas and I consider myself to be a 'lox and bagels' kind of Jew, rather than a religious kind of Jew."

"Is it hard for you in a mixed marriage?" Jessica asked.

"Not really. The older I get the more I do believe in God, and Daniel is an agnostic like I used to be, but I feel like I have more in common with him than I would with a really religious Jew. I think all religions are really about the same God, even if they do have different names or traditions about Him. I suppose my religion is primarily a personal spirituality, formed by a number of influences, just like my practice as a therapist is primarily eclectic rather than one specific type of therapy. To me, it seems like people have terrible wars over who has the better metaphors. No matter what you call God I can't imagine He is happy to see us killing each other over religion."

"No, I agree with you there. And what about your kids? Anna and I have been talking about how to raise Bridget, because I'm Protestant and she is Catholic, so I suppose that's why I'm so interested in you and Daniel. You kids seem to be so free of issues about this, and Stephen was easy because his dad and I both grew up in the same church. Not that we ever went to church, mind you."

"I'm not so sure my kids don't have issues about it. I suppose only time will tell. They have grown up getting Christmas ornaments as Chanukah presents, so I'm sure they'll grow up to join the *Church of the Religiously Confused*! But both of my parents were Jewish and I've been confused about my spiritual beliefs all my life, exploring all different kinds of religions, so what's the difference?"

"Yeah, I know what you mean. And what about Daniel? Doesn't he have any sort of tie to his Christian roots?"

"No. He says his most spiritual experience is looking through the telescope at night."

"Oh, that's so Daniel. Always the scientist."

"Isn't it? I think if he ever does find God he'll probably find Him on the Internet! But seriously, I think that Dan and I both agree about our basic values, and I think we've imparted those values to our kids from the beginning. When push comes to shove, I think that's what it's really about. Somehow I think the kids do have a basic Judeo-Christian value system, so I do feel good about that, at least on good days," Zoe said.

"For Anna and me a good day is one where we wake up and realize Bridget has slept through the night. So I guess we still have some time to think about this."

"Well, I have a one o'clock client, so I'd better go and review my notes from the last session. See you later, Jessie."

"Bye, and thanks for some interesting ideas. We can talk about Thanksgiving some more as it gets closer, so you can let me know what to bring," Jessica offered.

"O.K. Gotta run. Catch you later."

CHAPTER 5

Leah and the Barf Club

Thirteen-year-old Leah sat back, ripping open the Velcro straps on her sneakers and then neatly replacing them. With her grey-blue eyes she studied her mother, who was leaning back in the recliner reading the newspaper.

"Mom, I need your advice on something," Leah said, pushing back her fine blonde hair, trying to sound nonchalant. Zoe might have fallen out of her chair if she hadn't already been practically on her back.

Leah is asking advice from me? "Sure, Honey. What's up?"

"I'm worried about my friend Bizzy at school. I think she has an eating disorder. And I promised her I wouldn't tell anyone, but it's really gross and it's getting out of hand. I don't know if I should tell her mother. I think she has bulimia. That's the one where you vomit, isn't it?"

"Yes. Why? What makes you think so?"

"Well, there is this club at school that Serenity started, and Bizzy has joined up with the rest of the popular girls and that's what they do."

"What they do? What do you mean?"

"Throwing up. They have this throwing-up club. Can you believe it? I'm not supposed to tell anyone, Mom, but she really grossed me out when she was talking about it. She told me she went out with her vomiting group yesterday and they all went and got sundaes at Freddy's Restaurant after school. She said they got these huge sundaes with lots of gooey stuff on top and pigged out on them. Then, after they were done, Serenity decided who would go first to the bathroom to throw up. Serenity is sort of like the leader of this club that Bizzy is in, and she tells them who needs to get rid of stuff and who doesn't. They tell Serenity what they ate that day and then she tells them whether they need to go barf again or whether they don't. Bizzy says Serenity is getting more and more bossy about it. Yesterday she decided they all had to get rid of stuff in order to stay in the club on account of how huge these sundaes were. First, Bizzy said, Serenity sent Monica to make sure the coast was clear in the bathroom. It was. Then Serenity went first, then Jasmine, then Muffy, then Crystal, then Bizzy said she went last. It smelled pretty gross in there by that time, she said, so she didn't even have to stick her finger down her throat that time. She sounded all proud of herself telling me how now she can just smell the barf and think about barfing and then she can. 'I'm getting pretty good at that,' she says to me, like she's all proud of how easy it is for her to throw up. It's sick, and it's disgusting, Mom, but I promised her I wouldn't tell. And here I am telling. I feel like a tattle-tale."

"Leah, telling is not the same as tattling. You're a good friend and you're worried about her. You're not trying to get her into trouble. You are right to be concerned about her because this is not the kind of thing a friend can help with. She needs professional help, honey." Zoe pulled up the handle on the recliner as if springing to action. She contemplated the spectacle of a stream of adolescent girls binging and purging together in a club, traipsing back and forth, to and from the bathroom at Freddy's Restaurant. Zoe thought about how best to handle this so that Bizzy got help and Leah didn't feel betrayed.

"You don't belong to this club, do you Leah?" Zoe asked suddenly.

"Of course not. I'm not popular. I told you, you have to be popular to be in this club, and anyway, they have an initiation to get in. They blindfold you and make you eat this big bucket of nasty stuff and then you have to barf it all up in front of everyone. It's too disgusting for me."

"Good. I'm glad to hear it. But what do you mean, you're not popular, Leah? The phone is ringing off the hook here, other kids are always inviting you over, and you have a sleep-over party you go to almost every month. You have a lot of friends. Don't you consider yourself popular?"

Leah rolled her eyes. "God, Mom. That has nothing to do with it. You're only popular if you're popular with the popular kids. I have a lot of friends, but I'm only popular with the unpopular kids! Anyway, Mom, what should I do about this barf club thing? What if Bizzy finds out that I told? I really don't want her to know that I got her in trouble. She'll never speak to me again. I promised her I wouldn't tell, and I broke my promise."

"You're in a very tough spot, honey, but you're doing the right thing by telling me, and you are a doing what a good friend does. Is there anything else you haven't told me?"

"Yeah. Bizzy told me that when she makes herself throw up that there is blood coming up with it. That's when I knew I had to tell on her. I told her she has to tell her mom so she can go to the doctor but she won't and she won't stop making herself throw up, either. I'm really worried about her. Is she going to bleed to death?"

"No, honey, we'll see that she gets help."

"Are you going to call Bizzy's mother?"

"I don't think I'll call Bizzy's mother directly. I'm going to call Mrs. Moore, the school counselor, and tell her the whole story you just told me. Ashcroft needs to know that this is going on. It sounds like a lot of girls are involved in this. That way you'll be helping all of the girls, and not just Bizzy."

"Oh, God, Mom, you're not going to make a big thing about this at school, are you?" Leah asked, grabbing her mother's arm.

"No, Leah, I am not going to make a big thing about this at school. This is already a big thing. I think you know that and I think that's why you told me about this. Just trust that Mrs. Moore will take care of this without betraying your confidence. She is very sensible about these things."

"Yeah, Mrs. Moore is really cool."

"Do you feel comfortable with the plan, then, Leah?"

"Yeah, I guess so. But I wish you didn't have to call the school."

"I understand that, honey. But the situation you described is just too complex for you and the other kids to cope with on your own. Bulimia is a serious disorder with a number of major health consequences. Getting help for the girls involved is the most important thing we need to do."

"I only hope Bizzy doesn't wind up hating me."

"She might be angry if she finds out that you told on her, but I think that's a risk you have to take. You're doing the right thing, and that's what you need to do. I'm proud of you for recognizing that this was a problem you needed to talk to me about. That took a lot of courage, Leah. Do you have any idea how all of this got started?"

"I'm not sure, but I think it started after we measured our percentage of body fat in gym class. That's when everyone started talking about how fat they are. I think Serenity is the one who started it. She's the most popular of the popular kids, so the kids listen to her. I used to be really jealous of Serenity, Mom, because she gets a new outfit every single weekend. But you know what? I think that's why she is a spoiled brat who bosses everybody around. Her parents just throw money at her to get rid of her, like they're paying her to get lost and go to the mall. I feel kind of sorry for her. After all, it's not her fault if her parents are filthy rich. Maybe Mrs. Moore can help her too."

"I'm hopeful that she can. Do you feel OK about this now? Do you understand the plan of action?"

"Yeah, I guess so. I feel kind of relieved. Thanks, Mom."

"And I hope you heard how impressed I am that you had the courage to seek help for your friend. When you do the right thing it feels good all the way around."

"Don't go getting all lovey-dopey on me, Mom. Jeesh!" Leah shuddered as if to shake off Zoe's affection.

CHAPTER 6

Diana and Roz

Diana found herself thinking about how her counseling session had gone, and she decided to talk to Roz about it when they had lunch together at Piccadilly Pub. Diana liked the view of Fort Meadow Reservoir, and Roz really loved their food.

"So how did it go yesterday with your new counselor?" Roz asked before Diana was even able to raise the subject. Roz was never one to miss an opportunity to get to the point. Whenever Diana was unsure whether to call a client back, Roz always advised her to do it. "When you snooze, you lose," Roz would say, her sparkling brown eyes and her bouncy dark curls dancing in unison with her perpetually moving body.

"I'd tell you how it went Rozzie, but I don't know. It's like I felt both attracted to this therapy thing and revolted by it at the same time. I just don't want to get sucked into anything that's going to make me feel like there's something wrong with me. I want help but I don't want to need help. You know what I mean? I don't want to be one of those people who always has to call up their shrinks before they make every decision. And besides, she asks me the funniest questions and she phrases things in a strange way. I can't tell if it went well or not. It was really weird."

"Weird in what way?" Roz's direct and probing manner was what had made her a skilled recruiter.

"I don't even know how to explain it. It was like there was this feeling like everything was more important than it seemed to be on the surface. I kept thinking about it later, even though I really didn't want to be thinking about it. Remember when we were kids back in the seventies and we used to say 'heavy'? It felt like it was 'heavy!' in that 'wow, this is profound' kind of way. I felt so drawn to it. I felt like a moth drawn to a flame."

"That sounds kind of awful. Do you have to go back?"

"No, I'm cured in one session! Of course I have to go back. Besides, that's the other strange thing. I feel like I really want to go back, like I can hardly wait to go back. But then I feel like I really hated it there, too. Strange, huh?"

"To tell you the truth, Diana, it doesn't sound anywhere near as weird as those dreams you keep having. And aren't you going so the dreams will stop? Have you had any new ones?"

"Yeah, I did have a strange new one as a matter of fact. This really fat woman is sitting on a pillow with her belly sticking out like a big fat Buddha. All of these strange creatures from all over the universe are there, and I'm there too. I feel like Dorothy in Oz, because I'm sure as hell certain that we ain't in Kansas anymore."

"What do you mean, anymore? Have you ever even been to Kansas?" Roz got that mischievous grin that she displayed so often, revealing the dimples in her cheeks.

"Shut up, Rozzie! I'm trying to tell you this! So, anyhow, I go up to this really fat massively huge woman and I say, 'Where am I?' So she says, 'If you're with me, you're in India.' That's all I remember. I think she was wearing earphones or a Walkman or something, too. Then I woke up with a start. That's it."

"So now what do you do? Do you go ask Zenda the shrink what it means?"

"No! It doesn't mean anything. Besides, it isn't Zenda, it's Zoe."

"Whatever."

"Anyway, it was just a plain dream. It wasn't like those déjà vu psychic numbers that keep coming up. Actually, it was kind of fun to have a silly dream that was just a plain old dream. I suppose I could ask Zoe about it. She told me that she does dreams, but who cares what it means? It means I had a normal everyday silly dream and that's just fine with me. Maybe this therapy thing is helping already."

"See that! You ARE cured in one session! Zorinda the Wonder Shrink!"

"Zoe! I told you, it's Zoe."

"What in the hell kind of a name is Zoe? Besides, I don't think you should be afraid of those psychic dreams. They could be useful at work. You could start dreaming about which clients have search assignments for us and which candidates are open to new job opportunities. At least that would be useful."

"Didn't I ever tell you about my psychic placement?" Diana asked.

"I thought you'd told me everything but that one doesn't ring a bell." Roz smiled because she knew that Diana rang a bell to celebrate whenever she made a placement.

"This was back when I was doing office support placement in that little building over by the Royal Plaza Hotel before they knocked it down to build that bigger modern building. I went into the liquor store downstairs in the building to buy a lottery ticket. So the clerk in the liquor store tells me that his brother is a shipping and receiving guy who just got laid off, and he says, 'Since you're a headhunter, can you help get my brother a new job?' So I tell him that I don't place shipping and receiving people. But I get this really strong feeling that I'm supposed to call Erin, my contact in the human resources department. So I call Erin and she says, 'Your psychic powers are waning, Diana. We only have one shipping and receiving guy and he's been here for twenty three years.' We both laugh, and that's about it. Then Erin calls me back about three hours later. She says, 'You know, Diana, this is really getting scary.' So I say, 'What do you mean?' Then Erin tells me that two hours after I called her, their shipping and receiving guy quit and that now they have an opening. And that's how I wound up placing the liquor store clerk's brother with my best client. I got a nice little fee for it, too. That was back when I was making a lot of money before I became a nervous wreck basket case."

"Oh, puhlease, Diana! Spare me! You act like you're doing poorly now and you know that you aren't. Don't believe that story you're telling yourself. You will be making a lot of placements again soon. It'll turn around for you. It always does. You just need to believe in yourself."

"Spare me the goody two-shoes crap, would you Roz? It's not just a story I'm telling myself. It's the truth! I feel like I've gone from the King Midas touch to the King Mud Ass touch."

"Diana, Diana, Diana," Roz repeated slowly, shaking her head, as if she needed even more dramatic emphasis than her loud voice and gesticulating hands already provided. "You know you have a lot of stuff pending on your desk. Anything could come through at any time. We all have dry spells. You know that. It's the nature of the recruiting business."

"Well, my dry spell feels like a whole desert and every sign of water is like an illusion, an oasis in the desert that doesn't exist. I feel really shaken, like I've lost my confidence, and I'm worried that it's starting to show. Do I seem like a basket case to you, Roz?" Diana began crying, looking around the restaurant to make sure no one she knew was looking at her.

"No, you do not seem like a basket case! Anyone would be scared by those weird dreams coming true in real life. Really, Diana."

"I'm scared that the cure will be worse than the sickness. I don't know if I should go back to see Zoe again or if I should cut out of there before I start feeling too dependent on her."

"Look, go back and see her again. Then see how you feel after that. You can always quit later. But give it a try long enough to see if it could help you. You have been so upset by your dreams for so long, Diana. Maybe you could get some peace of mind. At least give it a long enough chance that you see if it can work."

"You're right. I should at least go back once more. I guess it's like we tell our candidates. 'Do you have enough interest in this opportunity to go back and gather more information about it so that you can make an informed decision?' I used to think that was just sales bullshit, but it really isn't. I've seen too many times when people like a place after a second interview that they didn't like on the first interview. Maybe therapy is like that too."

"I'll bet it is. First impressions are not always right. Give it time, just like we tell our candidates during our interviews. And speaking of interviews, we'd better get back to work now. Where in the hell is our waitress? I have a candidate out on an interview and I want to get back in time to hear how it went." Roz touched Diana lightly on the arm as the waitress slapped the check on the table. "Hang in there, Kiddo."

"O.K. Thanks, Roz. I really do feel better now. You always give me such good advice."

"I'm sorry, but our time is up. That will be $100 dollars, please.'

"Hey, no fair! Lucy only charges Linus five cents!" Diana protested.

"By the way, Diana, do you think about the money when you're there? Do you tell her something and then stop and think, 'That just cost me five dollars?'"

Diana laughed at this suggestion. "No, if I did that, it really would drive me nuts!"

CHAPTER 7

Tina and Joe

Tina was beginning to feel like a prisoner in her own home, plotting escape and dreaming of freedom while trapped by the fear of her husband, Joe. How had it come to this? There was no getting around it, Joe was jealous of his own son and the attention Tina gave to Joey. Tina remembered how sickened she felt when Joe had dislodged the baby from her nursing breasts in order to lick and suck on them himself. Sure, she had always babied Joe before little Joey was born. But she thought that he would be able to grow up once he became a father, and to see that her attention had to be focused on the needs of her son. Instead, he became more infantile, jealous of his own son for suckling at his mother's breasts. Joe considered Tina's breasts his property, and every moment Tina spent caring for their child was a moment lost to him. The verbal abuse started after the baby was born, too: the snide remarks, the unflattering comments about Tina's body being fat from the pregnancy, the daily barrage of niggling put-downs. Was the Joe she married the same man who now left her trembling, dreading the sound of his keys in the lock, signaling his return?

Tina thought back to the times when they were playful and had fun together. Joe used to chase Tina around their apartment, tickling her mercilessly once he caught up with her. Tina would grab cans of beer out of the refrigerator and put them down Joe's shirt for revenge, laughing, and saying, "Maybe this will cool you off!" Then the chase would begin again, with peals of their laughter punctuated by Tina's occasional squeals when Joe got too rough. Joe began to slap her on her arms, legs or bottom, often pretending to spank her. In fact, in the beginning, Tina had really liked the spankings, and found them an arousing ritual of sexual foreplay they shared. Joe would slowly take off all of Tina's clothes, moving his large hands over her smooth, soft, ivory skin. Then he would kiss her deeply, making hickeys on her neck or sinking his teeth lightly into her ear lobes. His breath would grow hotter and faster as he grabbed her breasts, licking her nipples until they stood at attention. Then Joe would rip his own clothes off and put Tina over his knee to spank her as Tina struggled and squirmed, trying to get away. Tina felt Joe's erection swell beneath her, and she felt her own breath quickening as her clitoris tingled in expectation.

Tina would tense the cheeks of her buttocks, trying to steel them against the onslaught of loud smacks that left them red and stinging for hours afterwards. Tina continued to squeal and struggle against the spankings, as she felt her vagina becoming wet and welcoming. "You've been a very bad girl," Joe would say, "and very bad girls need spankings." The spankings really stung, but the sex they had afterwards was so intense and frenzied, that Tina was able to achieve an orgasm for the first time ever. Tina was ecstatic to learn that she could feel pleasure from sex, and the spankings aroused her so much that she would beg Joe to enter her. The orgasms she had were blissful relief to pent up sexual tension which had developed over months of Tina lying still in bed, enduring Joe's frantic thrusting which left her sore and feeling nothing at all except frustration.

At first, it was the same kind of spanking every time and then they began to play out different roles and fantasies. Sometimes Joe was Daddy and Tina was the naughty little girl who needed to be punished. "You've disobeyed your Daddy," Joe would say, "and you know what happens next. Drop your drawers and bend over my knee!" Sometimes Joe was the principal and Tina was the errant schoolgirl who broke the rules and needed to learn a lesson. "Thought you wouldn't get caught. Let's see how many spanks it takes to make you to behave!" Joe would say sternly, as he counted the stinging smacks he delivered.

In their favorite fantasy, Joe played a cowboy, wearing nothing but a Stetson hat and cowboy boots with spurs. "Howdy, pardner!" Joe would say as he pranced around the room displaying an erection, looking at himself in the full-length mirror as Tina laughed. She was dressed only in frilly black lace panties and corset, her black net stockings held in place by a sexy red ruffled garter. Tina played the role of a saloon prostitute of the Old Wild West, pretending to "lasso" Joe's stiff penis, tossing her garter around it. Joe would gradually back up further and further as Tina threw the "lasso," and the spanking would start as soon as she missed. "So you think you can rope me in," Joe would say. "But you always miss. Seems to me that you're cruisin' for a bruisin'! I think you need your butt-naked ass whupped, you two-bit sassy slut!" Tina enjoyed this erotic fantasy until the day that Joe made a birch switch to use on his historical hussy. He struck her with such force that he drew more than blood. He drew an invisible line, and then he crossed it.

Soon after that, when the stimulating spankings became more and more like beatings, Tina blamed herself at first. Hadn't she been actively participating in these fantasy games which encouraged Joe to hurt her? Those stinging spankings turned her on like nothing else could. Over time, Tina grew sexually excited just at the sight of Joe's hat and boots. And Joe never really hurt her while he was sober, at least not before the baby was born. After Joey was born Tina realized that she was married to fear, and that fear grew even faster than her baby. Tina and Joe's sex life continued to include pain, but now there was no pleasure in it for Tina. Joe wanted sex again as soon as the baby was born and he became angry when Tina told him that the doctor said they should wait for six weeks. She knew it would hurt her, since she still had not healed from her episiotomy.

"C'mon my sassy slut. It's just like getting back on a horse," Joe had said, putting on his cowboy hat and holding his riding crop menacingly. Tina endured the intercourse, feeling raped as she listened to the spurs on Joe's cowboy boots knocking together with every painful thrust.

"Pardner, Doc Holiday has sewn you up nice and tight! Let's ride 'em again!" Joe didn't seem to notice the difference between Tina's facial contortions from orgasm and her wincing in pain and anguish. Night after night, Tina became tense, knowing she had to withstand ripping thrusts that left blood under the sheets and whippings that often left blood on top of them. She tried to fantasize about spankings like she used to do, so that the pain would turn her on, but it just didn't work that way any more.

She thought of leaving every day, but now she had an infant to consider. Tina felt overwhelmed when she thought of how vulnerable she had become. Eventually, she learned to stop thinking about it, holding on to the hope that Joe would change. She wanted to leave, but how would she support herself and Joey? She recognized the pitying stares of strangers whenever she went out in public, no matter how much make-up she used to try to camouflage her welts and bruises. Despite everything, Joe made good money, and she took some comfort in knowing that Joey, at least, had everything he needed.

CHAPTER 8

Diana's Dream Journal

$\mathcal{D}$iana watched the yellow leaves fluttering and falling in front of her car windshield as she drove to her appointment with Zoe. Canadian geese stretched out across the sky, and a farm stand decorated with corn husks and scarecrows displayed bins full of pumpkins. The fields of purple loostrife, which had carpeted the wetlands all summer, were still growing around the edges of Hager Pond, and the colored leaves of Autumn were still as vivid as her dreams.

Diana had been keeping a dream journal, writing down the strange stories that her mind created for her nearly every night. Diana found that she could best remember her dreams by getting into the same position she was in when she had dreamed them. It was awkward trying to write lying down, but her recall of the dreams was so much better when she stayed in bed to write. Engrossed in thinking of her dreams, Diana passed the Wayside Country Store and noticed the two benches out in front, one marked "Republicans" and one marked "Democrats."

Drat! I overshot it! She slowed down, turning the car around, passed the gazebo in front of Hager Pond, and drove into the parking lot at the counseling center. The red, salt-box colonial house, its steeply slanted roof dating it to at least three hundred years ago, was on Route 20, so it was not surprising that it had been converted to office space. Diana sat in the waiting room, looking at low ceilings, exposed wooden beams. The wide plank floors were worn by centuries of feet that had shuffled along them. She tried to imagine how the people would have looked in the olden days, when the house was built. She smiled as she realized that she was picturing classic Thanksgiving style Pilgrims reading the cartoons in the *New Yorker* magazines, waiting patiently for their therapists to show up. Zoe was escorting another client out and the white noise maker blocked out all but the sound of Zoe's laughter. Diana felt like Zoe was having a party and she wasn't invited. Soon enough, the party guest left and Zoe ushered Diana up the creaking stairs with a slight hand gesture and a welcoming smile.

Once in the session Diana opened her dream journal and got down to work right away.

"Wait until you hear this weird dream I had. It actually wasn't scary at all, it was funny and strange."

"Hmmm..."

"You know how I've been having these gruesome, ghastly dreams? I think I'm getting better already because this latest one, I just can't understand, but I liked it. I had a dream that I was in your waiting room. There was this incredibly nerdy man, who looked like a cross between Pee Wee Herman and Barney Fife. He was just sitting there, staring into space, not reading or anything. Then, in walks this really fat woman and she sits next to him. They're talking but I can't make out any of the words. In the dream, I really want to know what they're saying, but I can't hear them. Then the scene changes. That always happens in my dreams. There are different dream scenes and they switch up, and you can't remember how you got from one scene to the other. Anyway, all of a sudden they are in a bedroom together and I'm watching them have sex. The woman stops in the middle and says to me, 'What are you doing here?' And I say 'I'm waiting for

Zoe.' So she says, 'Waiting for Zoe is like waiting for Godot.' That's all I remember."

"What did you make of that?" Zoe asked.

"I don't know what to make of it. It is so rare that I have dreams about sex. It's normal, isn't it? It doesn't mean that I'm a pervert or anything, does it?"

"Perfectly normal. How did you feel in the dream?" Zoe asked.

"I was a little ticked off because I wanted to be in your waiting room, and instead I was with these two spazzy looking people."

"So you were feeling angry?"

"Angry? Oh no, not angry! I was just frustrated because I was supposed to be seeing you and you disappeared."

"Do you see any connection between the dream and our last session?"

"No, not really. What do you mean?"

"Well, last week I told you I would be taking a week of vacation soon. In the dream, you are waiting for me, but I'm not where I'm supposed to be. Do you see any connection there?"

"No, don't be silly! That's just a coincidence. The dream wasn't really about you, it was about these other people. You weren't even there. I wonder why I dreamed about those other people having sex?"

"That sounds like a good question. What do you think?"

"Maybe it means I'm horny. I was just glad nobody died in it. I'm just glad it wasn't a psychic dream. I wonder why I dreamt about sex? What does that mean?"

"It's your dream, Diana, and ultimately you are the expert about the symbols in your dream."

"Well, all I can think of are the words 'closeness and cuddliness.' Like I felt lonely and left out, and they got closeness and I didn't. I also remember feeling like I envied them because they were having closeness and I wasn't."

"Hmmm. And what did you make of 'waiting for Zoe is like waiting for Godot?'"

"I don't know. I don't even remember who Godot is." Diana said.

"There is a play, *Waiting for Godot,* by Samuel Beckett, about all of the characters waiting for Godot and he never shows up," Zoe said.

"A real play? How could I dream about a real play that I never even heard of? Maybe I did hear about it and I just don't remember it?"

"I think that's quite likely," Zoe said.

"Well, as long as this Godot guy doesn't die and wind up on the eleven o'clock news, he can barge into my dreams any time he wants to." Diana spent much of the rest of the session discussing issues at work, and how her anxiety made her hypersensitive to disappointment. "Zoe, it feels so unfair that my boss gets to go away to Hawaii for the week to a National Association of Personnel Consultants convention, all expenses paid, and I don't. After all the billing I've done for that company, you would think that they would pay for me to go too!"

"Yes, it's hard to be the one left behind. Have you been having any feelings about my up-coming vacation?"

"You deserve a vacation just like everybody else does."

"Well, that's true. But that isn't what I asked you. I asked you your feelings about it." Zoe said.

My God, she is conceited. She thinks the whole world revolves around her. "I don't think it will bother me at all. I'll be fine. I can talk to Roz for free, anyway. No, my only thought about your vacation is that I hope you have a nice time, and my only feeling is that I wish I got to go too! Can I stow away with you? No, just kidding. Don't worry. I won't pull a *What About Bob* on you. I won't show up on your doorstep like Bill Murray did in that movie when he went on vacation with Richard Dreyfuss. That was so funny!" Diana laughed too loud and too long at this. "I can go on my own vacation any time I want to, so I have no reason to envy you. Where did you say you were going again?"

"I don't believe I did say where I was going." Zoe said, smiling.

Diana waited for Zoe to tell her where she was going, but she didn't. "Well, have fun in East Oshkosh or wherever you're going, and wherever you go, don't worry about me," Diana said, hoping Zoe would. "God, I hope I'm not such a basket case that I would need to see you that one week. I mean, a week really isn't very long because a lot of people go away for two weeks, or even three weeks. It would be pretty selfish of me to only think of myself and not think about how much you probably need to get away from all of us."

"All of us?"

"All of us who see you. Probably some of the other people you see are really crazy and just couldn't handle you leaving when they depend on you, but good thing I'm fine and everything. But what if one of those scary things happened again and I couldn't get a hold of you because you were off?"

Diana was only half listening as Zoe explained the plan for emergency coverage, because she knew she wouldn't need it.

"It's only dreams and imagination, anyway," Diana said, feeling the lump in her throat swelling to the size of a hockey puck. "That's all it is. Like that song used to say, 'It's just my imagination running away with me.' Diana heard her voice crack as she said this. "I just had a funny thought," she said. "I just imagined that you said, 'Sweet dreams,' to me. My mom used to say that and so did my Grandma. Of course I had nightmares even when I was a kid, so I guess it doesn't really work that well when you say, 'Sweet dreams,' But when my mom and Grandma said it, I felt like it was going to work." Although Zoe leaned forward in her chair, a signal that the session was about to end, Diana felt alarmed when Zoe told her their time was up. She lingered at Zoe's door, holding onto the doorknob with a tense grip. "Maybe that Bob guy had the right idea," she said as she let go, and quickly turned to walk away so Zoe wouldn't see the tears that were brimming in her eyes. "Sweet dreams," she said to herself.

CHAPTER 9

A Birthday Party at the Wentworths

"Leah, would you please open the bags of chips and put them out?" Zoe asked. "And when you're done with that I need you to set out the veggie platter."

"Can't Rebecca do it?" Leah whined.

"Rebecca is vacuuming. Come on, now. Everyone pitches in." Zoe was struggling to get the corn silk off of her hands and into the trash, but it didn't seem to want to behave.

"OK. Can I use those really cool dishes shaped like Fall leaves that we always use at Thanksgiving?"

"That's a fun idea. I forgot we even had those things. Do you know where they are?"

"Yeah, they're right up here above the microwave where all of the other serving dishes are, see? Do you want me to put out the dip too?"

"Sure, honey, thanks."

"I love having parties. Is Daddy going to barbecue today even though he's the birthday boy?"

"Of course! What would a party be without Daddy's steaks? We're lucky the weather is cooperating."

"Good! I hope he used the good kind of sauce and not the other stuff. Did you pick up the cake from the bakery yet?"

"Yes, it's on the dining room table. See how nicely it came out? Steak, salad, corn on the cob, birthday cake and ice cream. This is going to be a feast. It isn't every day that Daddy turns 50!" Zoe realized she had been raising her voice only after she heard the whir of the vacuum cleaner stop.

"You're next, Mom!" Rebecca said as she came through the kitchen door.

"Oh, no! I refuse to turn 50. I'm going to $49.95 and after that I go on mark down."

"Denial is not just a river in Egypt, Mom," Rebecca said.

"Rebecca, come look at this chocolate cake Mom got for Daddy," Leah said. "Doesn't it look yummy? And look, it even has a picture of a computer on it with a mouse and a mouse pad just like a real computer. And Mom got candles in the shape of a five and a zero. She said fifty regular candles would be too much to fit on the cake."

"That's really cute. Dad will love it."

"Speaking of cute, Stephen Jenkins is coming to the party, Rebecca." Zoe said, deliberately trying to sound nonchalant.

"Cool! He is so hot! But I wish you would tell me these things ahead of time, Mom. I would have dyed my hair."

"Not again!" Leah said. "You change your hair color every week," Leah said.

"Shut up, Nerd Brain. It's my hair! Besides, I always keep it brown. I just like to try out different shades and highlights. Why should you care, anyway?"

"I don't care. I thought you were going out with that tall blond kid in the school band."

"Eric? He's history. Where have you been?"

"How come nobody ever tells me anything around here? Why did you break up?"

"He was too immature for me."

"Good. Maybe he would go out with me now. I thought he was so hot!"

"As if, Leah! He's seventeen. Why would he go out with an eighth grader? Get real! Where's Dad?" Rebecca asked.

"On the computer upstairs. Where else would he be? Isn't that where he spends his life? How come he never helps?" Leah whined.

"It's his birthday. Besides, he will be helping out plenty by cooking the steaks," Zoe explained.

"We did all the work, Mom," Rebecca said. "We always do all the work. Why do you defend him all the time? You tell us that in a family we all have to pitch in, but I never see him doing any cleaning."

"He does all the yard work, and maintains the cars."

"You're doing it again, Mom. You're defending him!"

"Hello!" Jessica and Anna had arrived, carrying birthday presents and a big Tupperware bowl.

"I know you said you didn't need anything, but I brought some fruit salad anyway. You didn't already make fruit salad, did you?" Jessica said.

"No, and we all love it. Thanks." Zoe perused the downstairs looking for any last minute tasks. "Leah, would you please put the vacuum cleaner away?"

"Why do I have to do it? Rebecca is the one who took it out," Leah asked.

"That's just the point, Leah. Rebecca did the vacuuming. Come on, now. We all need to cooperate."

"I don't get why you tell us whoever takes stuff out puts it away, but then I have to put away the vacuum cleaner she took out. That's not fair!" Leah complained.

"Here, let me do it. It's probably heavy and I'm stronger than you, Leah," Stephen said with a smile that revealed his dimples.

"That's so thoughtful, Stephen," Rebecca said. "Let me show you where it goes." Rebecca was hoping she could open the hall closet without something falling out on top of them. Leah shot Rebecca an angry glance.

"Would you like to come upstairs and play with my Play Station II?" Leah offered. "I've got some really cool games."

"Sure," Stephen said.

"I'll come too," Rebecca said, glaring right back at her sister.

Zoe heaved a sigh of relief as the kids left. Anna was just coming back in through the garage door, carrying the car seat with the baby still sleeping inside of it. "Cherish these moments," Zoe said to Jessica and Anna. "Enjoy her while she is still too young to talk!"

"Oh, believe me, we are," Anna said. "Although Stephen doesn't really talk to us either. You know the old story: 'Where did you go?' 'Out.' 'What did you do?' 'Nothing.'"

"Daniel," Zoe yelled up the stairs, "Jessica and Anna are here!"

"Before I forget," Jessica said. "I have something to tell you." Jessica pulled Zoe aside while Anna was changing the baby on the bathroom counter. "I think two of our clients are having a romance."

"Really? Who?"

"Remember the guy I presented during Peer Supervision that time we were the only ones there? Nestor Pewkes?"

"The one who's still living with Mom?"

"Yes. Well I saw him with your client at the movies the other night."

"What client?"

"The obese woman who always used to be in the waiting room at the same time I see this guy: Wednesdays at seven. I thought I had spotted her giving him the once over when I came out to get him. But I never thought he would be able to respond. You told me you had to stop seeing her because her insurance company cut her off? They seemed to be quite the couple. He had his arm around her and everything. I'll tell you, she looked absolutely wedged into the theater seat. Anyway, I'm pleased about it. I really didn't think he'd be able to connect with anyone this soon."

Zoe realized that Jessica could only be referring to India Backus. *Wait a minute! Something about this sounds so familiar.* Zoe struggled to remember where she had heard this before. Diana's dream! The really fat woman and the geeky looking guy having sex. Again it was one of her other clients, and this time there was no chance that Diana could have overheard anything. She hadn't seen India since last summer! Zoe felt the hairs raise up on the back of her neck as she realized that Diana had foreseen this in her dream. Just then, Anna returned with little Bridget and Daniel finally came downstairs, ending their discussion about clients.

"So here's the old man himself," Jessica teased. "How are things where you are, Daniel, you know, over the hill?"

"Pretty much the same as they are on your side of the hill. I don't feel any different than I did yesterday!"

"Yes, but you're fifty now. Doesn't that bother you?" Anna asked.

"I'm still only one day older than I was yesterday. Why should it bother me?"

"Men!" Zoe said. "You gotta love 'em!"

"No, actually, we don't," Anna quipped, hugging Jessica. "It's you straight women who 'gotta love 'em.'"

CHAPTER 10

Tina And The Blessed Virgin

*T*ina sat in one of the empty pews of the large brick Immaculate Conception Church in downtown Marlborough. She felt safe in the sanctuary of the church, not because she felt the protection of a loving God, but because Joe would not come after her there. Tina also felt some small comfort from the beauty of this sacred place. The soft glow of the votive candles, the beautiful morning light that shone through the stained glass windows and the smell of incense brought her back to her childhood faith. She remembered clutching the rosary beads that her mother had given her for her First Holy Communion, the same beads that she now kept hidden in a small porcelain vase and grasped too tightly whenever she could steal away to say her prayers in private. She was still holding on to them, like a lifeline, even now. Only, now, those beads were all she had left of Mama.

Whenever Tina remembered the sense of safety she had during her childhood, she always wondered how that safety could have transformed so quickly into the terror she now knew. What kind of childhood would Joey have, lying awake in his room listening to the outrageous accusations, the desperate denials of wrongdoing, the sound of the blows delivered to his mother, their almost silent target?

Tina looked up at the statue of the Blessed Virgin, seeking tranquility in her smooth, enduring marble face. *Mother Mary, is God punishing me? If He is, what have I done wrong? How can this much pain come to me through the Blessed Sacrament of marriage? How can I leave Joe when divorce is a sin? Holy Mother, give me strength and deliver me from evil. Hail, Mary, full of grace, the Lord is with thee. Blessed art thou amongst women and blessed is the fruit of thy womb, Jesus. Holy Mary, Mother of God, pray for us sinners, now and at the hour of our death. Amen. Thank you for your intercession on my behalf, Holy Mother.*

As if in answer to this prayer, Tina suddenly remembered what Mama said to her one day when they were watching a made-for-TV movie about domestic violence. "Don't ever let this happen to you. If you are ever in a marriage like this, leave the son-of-a-bitch." Joey was three now, and Tina was still with Joe, still trying to find the courage to leave. Now she was exactly where she swore she would never want to be, living in the Land of Fear. Would she be able to heed Mama's advice and leave the son-of-a-bitch? Tina remembered the business card, and the whispered directive of Maria, little Rico's mother at the library story hour. "Call this woman. She'll help you. I know what's going on. It happened to me too."

Is it time for me to give up on Joe ever changing? Is it too late for our marriage? The Blessed Virgin only smiled. Tina thought back to the latest ugly incident and their conversation yesterday afternoon. Joe had been guzzling down one beer after another as he watched the ball game on TV. She remembered her heart racing, fear striking like a piano chord that was resonating even now. *What was it that scared me so much? Oh, sweet Jesus, I remember, he has a gun!*

"What are you doing?" she had asked.

"I'm sick of watching those squirrels all over my yard. God-damned rodents!"

"What? So what are you going to do, shoot them?" Tina blanched.

"How did you catch on to that one so quick, Dumbelina Tina?"

"You're not serious, are you?"

"You're damned straight I'm serious. Those squirrels are not going to infest my yard and take whatever they damn well please and think they are going to get away with it."

"But Joe, they are just doing what squirrels do. They're gathering nuts for the winter."

"Well, they gathered one nut for this winter that they didn't count on! And now there won't be any more winters for them." That sick, twisted laugh again.

"But Joe," Tina had said, using whatever she could think of to try to get Joe to stop, "you'll wake up Joey and I just got him settled down for his nap!"

"Well, isn't that just tough shit? Are you saying I can't have any fun because of little Joey? Nice try, bitch! Now get out of my way, or I'll shoot you too!" Joe pushed Tina with such force that she almost lost her balance. Joe then headed into the yard and began shooting his BB gun at the squirrels. Tina had felt helpless as she watched the carnage. But what disturbed Tina the most was that Joe laughed whenever he shot a squirrel, and he'd shot several of them. Tina felt her stomach churning as Joe returned to the apartment with a satisfied grin.

"I guess that takes care of that," Joe said, beaming. "Now bring me another beer and some pretzels. A man works up quite an appetite when he's out hunting."

"Okay. But can you at least get rid of the bodies? I don't want Joey coming across a dead squirrel in the yard when he's out playing."

"Why not? Just tell him that his Daddy is a great hunter. Maybe I should get one of them stuffed and give it to Joey. He likes stuffed animals, doesn't he?" Joe laughed again, while Tina cringed.

Tina looked up from these dark images to see the smile on the face of the Virgin was enduring still. She felt the worn business card in her pocket that she had been rubbing like Aladdin's lamp, hoping for deliverance. *Thank you, Mary. I understand. I know what I'm sup-*

posed to do now. Pray for me. Tina blessed herself with holy water as she left the sanctuary, glancing furtively at her watch, praying that big Joe and little Joey were still asleep at home. If she got home, quietly changed into her robe, and started cooking bacon, Joe would never need to know that she had gone to church. It was just too early in the morning for Joe's accusations. And it was just too late for their marriage.

CHAPTER 11

Diana and the Ormonds

*D*iana sat up in bed at three o'clock in the morning and gasped as she pulled off her flannel nightgown. She felt hot, sweaty, and clammy. This nightmare was worse than most of the others, although no one actually died in it, which was some consolation. *Wait until Zoe hears this one!* Diana got up out of bed and pulled a light summer nightie out of her dresser drawer and donned it. *Luckily, I don't have to wait long. Thank God I'm seeing her later today.* Diana got back in bed and tried to fall asleep, but kept remembering how the little boy felt. *I was actually thinking his thoughts in the dream, but he was almost too young to have any thoughts. I wonder why I was a little boy in the dream and not a little girl. I can't even remember how I knew I was a little boy, I just did. Actually, it was more like I was feeling his feelings. I have so many different feelings, I feel like I'm going to drown in them. I don't know how much more of this I can take!* Diana's heartbeat was still knocking on the door of her chest, keeping her awake and agitated. *I'm going to die of a heart attack. My heart won't stop pounding. His feelings were so gripping, so heavy and terrible. Who is he? I hate this feeling of being afraid to fall back to sleep. There's no rest for the weary, even in bed...*

"Beep! Beep! Beep!" Diana was surprised to be awakened by the sound of the alarm clock, since she was certain she would not be able to fall back to sleep. It seemed like no time at all had passed, but the alarm went off at six as usual, and Diana realized she must have fallen back to sleep after all. For the rest of the day she functioned on automatic pilot, counting the hours, then the minutes until she could get to Zoe's office. She could hardly remember the entire workday, except for the hug Roz gave her as she left the agency. She almost pounced out of her chair when Zoe came down the stairs to get her in the waiting room.

"So, what's up?" Zoe said, as she closely examined Diana, looking to read her facial expression, her body language, and listening closely to hear the tone of her voice.

"Oh, my God!" was all Diana could say. Zoe waited patiently, as Diana heaved heavy sighs, which punctuated the silence. "This dream I had…" Diana began to cry softly, put her head in her hands, and then looked up briefly at Zoe through tear-brimmed eyelashes.

"Another tough dream," Zoe said softly.

"I was just a little kid. Just a terrified little kid and they wouldn't stop. I could hear my mother crying, screaming for mercy, only I wasn't me and my mother wasn't my mother. You know how dreams are weird like that. I was in bed and the walls were so thin."

"Hmmmm. You were just a terrified little kid…" Zoe cooed empathically.

"I could hear everything. I was a boy, too. I don't know how I know that, I just know I was a boy, though. And I was so little and helpless and scared. I was praying that they'd stop fighting and hollering, but they didn't. He was roaring like a beast and she was whimpering, like an injured puppy. And the horrible sound of him hitting her! I felt like I saw their faces even though I couldn't see their faces at all. I think I was wearing a diaper because they were afraid I would wet the bed again. I remember the feeling of how uncomfortable it was. I was a boy in a diaper. I hate these dreams. I swear to God, I hate these dreams. Why do I keep having them?"

"I think that's a good question. What do you think?" Zoe asked.

"She is really in danger. She really has to get away from him or he's going to kill her and me too. Why am I a boy? I just can't shake this feeling. The poor little boy. He's even afraid to let them know he's afraid. She's trying to protect him, his mother is, but it's not going to work. The father is so much more crazy than she thinks he is. She's in danger. Real danger. What did you ask me?" Diana lifted her head up briefly and looked at Zoe.

"What it means to you that you keep having these frightening dreams," Zoe said.

"Oh, yeah. I don't know. Do you think it's another premonition? I don't even know who these people are or even where they are. I just have this feeling like they're in danger. I'm supposed to warn them, warn me, the little boy and his mother."

"Tell me more about the sense of danger you had in the feelings you felt."

"It was like being trapped. Being stuck. I was in danger, but I couldn't move. The phrase I keep thinking of is 'paralyzed by fear'. There I am stuck in my bed, afraid to go out because he might kill me too. I'm so tired of being afraid. I jump at the slightest noise. What if this proves I have more psychic powers? But how can I warn them if I don't even know who they are?"

"Who is it you need to warn?" Zoe asked quietly.

"Me, I mean the little boy that's me in the dream." Diana furrowed her brow.

"I see," Zoe said. Diana noticed that Zoe's eyes had widened like she was paying more and more attention to the dream. "You know, it strikes me that this little boy in the dream is in the same predicament you're in right now. He's afraid of how vulnerable he is to being hurt. He's scared, he's anxious, and he doesn't know what to do next. Does that seem familiar to you?"

"Yes. It's familiar. It's how the little boy felt in the dream last night. I think what I'm supposed to do is rescue him, or at least warn his mother so that she can rescue him. But I can't control my powers so I don't know how."

"And he can't control his vulnerability enough to protect himself. How could you help him? What would you say to him right now if he were here?"

"I'd tell him, 'Get out now while you still have a chance.'"

"Would he feel soothed and comforted by that?"

"No, I think it would scare him even more, but at least he would be safe if he listened."

"It is important to feel safe," Zoe said. "How could you help him with that?"

"I could only help him if I rescued him, otherwise he's just stuck there with no way to get out."

"What does he need to help him become unstuck?" Zoe asked.

"He needs a grown-up he can trust who can take care of him," Diana answered.

"Could the grown-up part of you help him with that?" Zoe asked.

"No. That's just it. I don't see how I could help him."

"You can't envision that yet," Zoe said.

"So what do I do?" Diana asked, her voice filled with desperation.

"Give him some time, and just sit with him and his feelings. Perhaps he'll feel more safe as time goes on."

"Perhaps he'll be more dead as time goes on too! I just don't know if it can wait! I think it might be too late already!" Diana was trembling as she looked pleadingly at Zoe.

"You're afraid for him." Zoe's voice was almost as soft as a whisper.

"Of course I'm afraid for him! Is this psychic thing just seeing things before they happen or are these powers making them happen? I'm scared that I'm causing them to happen, like *Carrie* at the prom or something. You know, Stephen King? I feel like if I could stop seeing it I might be able to stop it from happening, but I don't know how to stop seeing it. You keep asking me questions like you think this dream is about me or something, but you have to realize how much worse it is than that. If it were about me, if it were just a regular dream to analyze like normal people have, that would be one thing. But do you get that not knowing if this is real life or not is ruining my life? It's turning me into a nervous wreck! Sure, it's great to just turn over in bed and tell yourself that it's just a crazy dream, and go back to sleep. But ever since the dead people in Arkansas, I don't have that luxury anymore. I mean, how can I do that when this might be real people who are in immediate danger? What am I supposed to do, just let the kid and his mom get murdered by this lunatic? Just wait to see them in zippered-up body bags on the six o'clock news like all the others? Of course I have to warn them! But how do you warn them when you don't really know who they are or where they are? I feel like I shouldn't be here wasting time with you, I should be talking to the police. But what am I going to tell them, 'I had this dream last night and I don't know who the characters are but you have to go save them?' They'd probably put me in a straight jacket." Diana suddenly noticed that her voice had gotten loud and shrill. "I'm sorry. I'm yelling at you, like it's your fault."

"It sounds to me like you might be feeling some angry frustration with me and the work we're doing together. Your feelings are very raw and urgent. You may be wondering if the therapy can help you with them quickly enough to alleviate your suffering," Zoe said, matter-of-factly.

"No! Don't you understand? I am not angry with you! I just want to help those other people!" Diana dug her top teeth into her lower lip.

"If you did feel angry with me, would that be okay with you?"

"No, it wouldn't."

"What would it mean to you?"

"It would mean that I'm blaming you for all my problems, and I know you're only trying to help me!"

"Your anger is welcome here, along with all of your other feelings," Zoe soothed.

"Even if I'm feeling like this therapy thing just might be a giant crock of shit?"

"Even if you're feeling like this therapy thing just might be a giant crock of shit."

CHAPTER 12

Zoe and Daniel

Zoe breathed a sigh of relief when she realized that she would have a rare weekend alone with Daniel. Rebecca and Leah were staying at a hotel in Boston with a group of kids from Youth Pro Musica and a parent chaperone. They were going to be spending the weekend in rehearsals for a holiday concert with the Boston Pops at Symphony Hall. Zoe had almost volunteered to be one of the parent chaperones until Rebecca said, "God, Mom, no. How embarrassing!" Zoe also wanted to give Daniel some "Special Alone Time." Zoe and Daniel had come up with the idea of doing "Special Alone Time" with the kids whenever the sibling rivalry was getting too intense. She or Daniel would spend a day alone with one of the girls who could choose whatever activity they wanted. Zoe thought about how often lately Daniel had complained about her being unavailable and she wanted to attend to his needs, too.

Daniel playfully splashed some water on Zoe over the top of the shower door as she approached.

"Hey, cut that out!" Zoe said, stepping back a little.

"Cut what out?" Daniel said, feigning innocence.

"We have the weekend all to ourselves. What would you like to do for our 'Special Alone Time?'" Zoe had to raise her voice a bit to be heard over the sound of the water.

"Well, we could spend the weekend alone."

"No, really, Daniel."

"Really."

"Where do you want to go and what do you want to do?"

"I want to go out and I want to do something."

"Like what?"

"Well, whenever I'm not sure what I want to do, I always go back to bed to think it over." Daniel turned off the water and stepped out of the shower.

Zoe recognized this as an invitation. "I'm already dressed."

"Well, we could take care of that pretty fast." Daniel started shaking his head back and forth like a dog drying its coat, so that all the water in his hair splashed Zoe again. Zoe stepped back and gasped in mock alarm.

"What a shame! Your clothes are all wet. I'm afraid you're just going to have to take them all off," Daniel said, smiling broadly.

Zoe laughed. "Yes, I'm afraid I will." She started to disrobe as she sang *The Stripper*.

"Can you make a basket?" Daniel asked as he bundled up his towel and threw it into the hamper across the room.

"Sure!" Zoe said, tossing her balled-up clothes into the hamper one garment at a time, only missing once.

"Now I'm afraid you'll catch a cold if you don't jump right into this bed with me," Daniel said as he jumped under the comforter.

Zoe relaxed into Daniel's smiling eyes. "And we wouldn't want that to happen, would we?" she said.

"I'm only thinking of your health, of course."

"Of course," Zoe said as she began scratching his back and kissing the back of his neck.

"You know what I think is an important part of good health?" Daniel asked.

"What would that be?" Zoe asked.

"Rigorous physical exercise. The more rigorous the better."

"We do have to get our exercise. Let's see. What rigorous physical exercise could we do while we're in this bed, making sure we stay warm and don't catch cold?" Zoe was smiling warmly.

"I wouldn't know. Perhaps you could make some suggestions."

"Well, we could start with some warm-ups and go from there."

"An excellent idea!" Daniel said. Daniel began exploring Zoe's body with his hands, lingering at her nipples and gradually working his way down to her clitoris. Zoe felt herself becoming aroused as she began to pleasure Daniel, gently caressing the head of his penis. Zoe welcomed the smell of him, the touch of him, and all of him as they melted into the familiarity of each other. Their rigorous exercise rewarded Zoe with multiple orgasms, as the pleasure cascaded, coming to crescendo again and again. Of all of the communication they had, this wordless bonding was the most profound.

When they were finished, Zoe complimented Daniel, saying, "You know, you're so good at that, that I think you actually qualify as a health nut. In my professional opinion, of course."

"And you are an expert on all kinds of nuts, aren't you?"

"Why, yes I am!" Zoe laughed, as she rubbed the hair on his belly.

"Well, I'd have to say that you're so accomplished at that particular form of exercise that you are positively athletic."

"I'm so glad we work so hard at staying healthy," Zoe said, giggling.

"Well, of course, it is a lot of effort, but we have to make the sacrifice for the sake of our health." Daniel kissed Zoe again.

"I'm so glad I married you, Daniel, and I'd do it again in a heartbeat." Zoe snuggled closer to him.

"An excellent form of cardiac care, I'd say," Daniel said.

"Yes, love is always good for the heart." This time Zoe kissed Daniel and relished the sweet silence between them until she broke it by asking about plans for the day. "Seriously, Daniel, where would you like to go today?"

"I wouldn't like to go anywhere seriously."

"Come on!"

"I already did."

"Daniel!" Zoe said, hitting him over the head with her pillow.

"I was thinking of going into Cambridge and spending the day browsing in book stores. What do you think?"

"That sounds great," Zoe enthused.

"We could also have lunch over there at one of those hotels that overlooks the Charles River."

"Great. I love watching the sail boats and rowing crews from Harvard and MIT on the river."

"O.K. That sounds like a plan. I'll look up restaurants on the 'net while you get dressed." Daniel said, as he got out of bed to return to cyberspace, where he spent so much of his time.

Zoe smiled. *It's going to be a good day.*

CHAPTER 13

Zoe and Jessica

*J*essica Lakewood looked over at Zoe during Peer Supervision and noticed she had that zealous look on her face that Jessica had come to recognize. "You look like something's bothering you," Jessica said, as soon as the meeting broke up.

"Something's bothering me. I have a new client who is presenting with psychic dreams as her primary problem. She is afraid she has 'powers' as she puts it."

"It sounds to me like she really doesn't know how to tell you yet what her primary problem is. Lots of clients have fear of their own power. Do you think her dreams about having psychic powers could be a metaphor for that?"

"Possibly. I haven't been working with her long enough to know that, but that does make sense. She seems very committed to her work and has a lot bubbling up from her unconscious. Her fear of her magical powers is an interesting and unusual presentation. I wonder if she feels she has to be extraordinary in some way in order to engage my attention. Perhaps she's been abandoned in the past and learned that the only way she can get and keep attention is by being flamboyant and histrionic. I should be careful not to play into that. I need to let her know that she can get my attention just by being ordinary. She doesn't have to entertain me with wild stories to earn my attention. She needs to know that she deserves my attention just for being who she is, a unique individual. I'll have to be careful though, because I can feel that I really am drawn to all of this psychic stuff. I have a feeling that she didn't feel heard or understood."

"That doesn't sound like you," Jessica replied. "Most of your clients feel very heard and understood by you."

"How do you know that?"

"I can tell just from listening to the way you present cases in Peer Supervision. I'm sure your nurturing supportiveness is almost always felt by your clients."

"Thank you, that's so good to hear, and I hope you're right about that. It's a strange case. When this client said she thinks she's psychic and has magical powers, I was pretty quick to pooh-pooh it. I felt like she was working very hard to try to entertain me with ghost stories and I wanted to reassure her that her every day life was interesting enough."

"That makes sense."

"But I'm concerned that she may have felt I was discounting her feelings. When she left the session, she gave me a look and I've been thinking about that look all week. She may not come back."

"Well, she'll either come back or she won't, and either way you can stop wondering." Zoe could always count on Jessica for a logical viewpoint.

"It's very strange because I also somehow feel caught up in her mysteriousness. The other day I could have sworn she told me the same story I then heard from another client, later that day. It was uncanny. I was about to refer to our earlier conversation until I realized the earlier conversation wasn't with her, it was with my new psychic dreamer."

"You've been very busy lately. I find that when I become befuddled by the end of the day, it sometimes indicates that I'm seeing too many clients and it's all becoming a blur. Do you think that could be going on? Or are you questioning whether or not this psychic client is out of touch with reality?"

"She seems very rational until she gets into this psychic stuff. But I'm not sure yet. It's more like I'm beginning to wonder if she's more in touch with reality than the rest of us."

"Most of the time you can go with your gut. But if you join with her around her delusion, you're likely to get stuck, so I don't think that's where you want to go. It sounds to me like she is delusional, and I think you have to be firmly planted in reality in order to help her."

"Thanks, Jessie. That's sounds like good, solid clinical advice."

"And if you do get stuck inside her delusional system, don't worry, I'll come in there and bring you back to reality with the rest of us."

Zoe laughed. "O.K. If I start getting magical powers too, you'll be the first to know it."

"Boy, I'll tell you, I wish I'd have had some magical powers myself last night. Bridget is colicky and she is miserable! She was up crying half the night. Anna and I were taking turns walking her, rocking her, rubbing her back, and everything, but she wouldn't stop crying. The only one who slept through the night was Stephen. Of course, it's amazing he can still hear, the way he plays his music so loud. They may be at two very different developmental stages, but they both make a racket! How are things going with your family?"

"Fine. The girls and I went out to my parents' house in California for Rosh Hashona, the Jewish New Year, recently. The girls helped my mom bake a honey cake and a *kugel*."

"Oh, I love *kugel*! I remember when you made that noodle pudding for a pot luck we had at the office once."

"The kids love it, too, although Rebecca always picks out all the raisins. You know, it gave me such a good feeling to see the girls and their *Bubbe* cooking together. After dinner, Leah played the piano and she and Rebecca sang duets. My dad taught them a lullaby he used to sing to me in Yiddish when I was a little girl. It actually brought tears to my eyes. Leah played Chopin's "Nocturne" and I could tell my parents were *kvelling*."

"Mama said, 'If Chopin himself could hear this, he wouldn't be ashamed.'"

"That sounds so nice. You know, I always thought that the Jewish people had the right idea celebrating the New Year in the fall. September always feels like the beginning of a new year, maybe because the school year starts then. And it must be so great to see your parents passing on traditions to your children."

"Yes, especially since Daniel isn't Jewish and the kids aren't really exposed to it all that much. My parents always lay it on thick when we visit. They feel like they have to teach the kids all about the Jewish traditions. I know they were disappointed that I didn't marry somebody Jewish, but they love and respect Daniel and they can see how happy we are as a family. Anyway, we had a great time, and It was a wonderful visit, but it was painful to watch my father struggling to walk. He says his doctor wants him to get a hip replacement, but he's afraid to have surgery. Dad was putting an extra leaf in the table and he wasn't strong enough to pull it out far enough to put the leaf in. Rebecca jumped in to help her Zayde pull. Mom and Dad are both ailing and failing, but my mom still insists on having Rosh Hashona at home and cooking enough food for an army."

"Did Daniel go too?"

"No, he had too much to do at work, finishing up on some project."

"Well, I'm glad you had a nice vacation and a chance for your kids to connect to their Jewish roots. I gotta get going. I have an eleven o'clock."

"Okay. Well, thanks for the consult on my psychic dreamer and I'll let you know how it plays out."

CHAPTER 14

Tina and Zoe

Zoe looked over the petite, dark-haired young woman who was sitting on the office couch twisting the fringe on one of the pillows. Her facial features were even and almost attractive, but there was a haunted quality to her. She had been so evasive over the phone with the Intake Department that Zoe had little idea what was prompting her to seek therapy. Zoe remembered a vaguely paranoid flavor to her during the initial call, but she knew little about her new client, who told her she didn't want to say anything over the phone. "How may I be useful to you?" Zoe asked quietly.

Tina burst into tears, occasionally punctuated by repeating "I'm sorry," while Zoe waited. Tina heaved a long, shaky sigh before she began her anguished tale. "I need someone to help me to get away. I know I need to do it, but I can't. And I'm not really sure what I should do. We made vows at our wedding and I promised to take him 'for better or for worse.' It's mainly been worse, but divorce is a sin, and I don't want Joey to grow up without a family."

"It sounds like there's been quite a struggle for you. What prompts you to consider ending your marriage at this time?"

"I think my husband is going to kill me." Tina looked around furtively as she said this, as if checking for spies.

"You don't feel safe with your husband."

"Safe? I'm not sure I even remember what it feels like to be safe with anyone. See, sometimes he hits me, but not all the time. Usually, it's only when he's been drinking. But then again, sometimes he's so sweet. He bought me a big box of chocolates for Valentine's Day. I always wanted someone to give me a heart-shaped box of chocolates for Valentine's Day. To me, that was the most important sign of love. Then he did, so I changed my mind about leaving him for a while. I keep making up my mind that I want to leave him, but then he goes back to being so good to me. He begs me to forgive him and he tells me he'll never do it again. No matter how many times it happens, I always believe him. He sounds so sincere, like he's really going to try this time. And he does try. It's just that he always loses it again."

"And what have you lost?"

"I've lost a lot. I've lost my mind. That's the only explanation for why I haven't left him yet. Now, even when I pray, I feel like I should leave. I feel like God wants me to leave, even though divorce is a sin, because murder is a bigger sin. I keep wondering what will happen to little Joey after Joe kills me?"

"That sounds like an important question for you to be asking yourself."

"So far, I've stayed with him because of Joey. But recently, he's gotten crazier. He was really close to his mother and she committed suicide a few months ago. After that, it was like he hardened. Like his mother was the only light in his world and after she died, everything turned black for him. He's gotten so mean and cold now, even when he's not drunk. He used to only beat me when he was drunk, and sometimes I could get him to stop. It didn't happen more than a few times a year. But after his mother died, it's like he turned into somebody else. Now there's this cruel streak in him that scares me. I keep thinking that if I just love him enough, if I could just be the light in his life that his mother used to be, that he would change. I promised to love him but I don't know how anymore. Maybe he could change, though."

"How successful has he been at changing so far?"

"He's mainly changed for the worse."

"So while you've been working hard to be a good mother to your son and a good wife to your husband, he hasn't been working on changing at all. Instead, you've been working on changing him."

"I never thought of it that way. When you put it that way, it sounds kind of hopeless."

"Hmmm," Zoe hummed in agreement. "You can decide to change your own behavior. But you can't decide to change somebody else's behavior. It doesn't work that way."

"I want to leave him, but I can't."

"What's stopping you from doing what you know you need to do to protect yourself and your son?"

"I'm scared. If he finds us trying to get away he's going to kill us. If we stay, he will keep beating me, but I'm not sure he'll kill me if I stay. He needs me. And he loves me, too."

"He loves you?"

"I know it sounds warped, but I do think he loves me. But I still have to leave him. The last time I went to the hospital after he beat me I was so broken up that I was afraid he'd kill me the next time whether I stayed or not. He broke my jaw, he broke my nose, he broke a rib. He keeps telling me I deserve it, and sometimes I think I do. I tell myself that I know what I need to do to be a good wife and if I would just do better he wouldn't have to beat me. But lately, sometimes I think no one deserves what he's done to me, no matter what they've done. He's broken me like you break an animal. I need to get away, but I can't. He'll track me down like an animal, too. I feel like there's no escape but death." Tina began weeping again, while Zoe pondered possible escape plans. Tina's escape would be no small undertaking. Batterers are often most dangerous when women seek to escape them, so it would have to be managed carefully to avoid putting Tina and Joey at risk.

Zoe was alarmed when Tina seemed to minimize and justify the very real danger she was in, which had prompted her to seek Zoe's help in the first place. Like Venetian blinds, which alternately let in light and then block it again with a snap, Tina vacillated between seeing her own predicament, and not really seeing it. "Tina, what options do you see for yourself?" Zoe asked.

"I could leave him and find a job," Tina said in a tentative and questioning voice, "but who would want me? I don't think I could get a job. I don't know how to do anything. Joe tells me all the time how useless I am. I don't think anyone else would ever put up with me. I have to protect Joey, but if I were to leave Joe to go to work, I couldn't afford both the day care and all the expenses of living. Besides, Joe makes all the money and he can be really sweet sometimes, even now, and he really loves Joey."

"Will Joe be sweet next time before or after you're dead?"

Tina sat back against the couch cushion as if pushed by the impact of the question. Zoe studied Tina as she flattened herself against the back of the couch, unable to answer the question. Tina was trembling so much that it seemed that she was having a hard time holding herself together. "Rattle trap" popped into Zoe's mind. Tina opened her mouth as if to speak, twice and then gave up and sat in silence for a few minutes.

"There are no words," Zoe said.

Tina continued crying, then asked, "What if we came in for marriage counseling. Would that work?"

"No. Unfortunately, what our research shows is that the best treatment in a situation like this is to provide safety for the victim and prosecution for the perpetrator. When batterers are put in jail, sometimes they stop battering. They may not be able to consider the feelings of other people, but they will sometimes stop if they fear consequences to themselves. If the negative consequences to them are severe enough, they are sometimes able to change their behavior in order to avoid more punishment. Often, however, they are not."

"So you think he could change?" Tina asked hopefully.

"I think his changing is unlikely. If he were the one sitting in front of me saying, "Do you think I can change?" there might be some chance that he could. But my guess is that he believes that you have problems and that he doesn't. Am I right?"

"Yes. He tells me that if it weren't for me being such a lousy wife he wouldn't have to beat me. He even blames me for the cost of the hospital visits and says that if I weren't such a sorry ass loser that we could pay off all the cards. He took my credit cards away and put me on an allowance. Now I can barely afford to feed Joey and buy him new clothes when he outgrows them."

"He seems to fit the usual pattern of domestic violence perpetrators very well. It's all about power and control issues. They want to have more and more power over you and they try to control you by limiting your access to supportive people in your life and to resources like money and transportation. Tell me, has he limited your access to your friends and family?"

"Yes! How did you know? He won't let me see my friends anymore. He says that I don't need to go anywhere and when I do he calls me a slut for sleeping around. He makes these wild accusations. How he thinks I could be having all of these affairs while I take care of little Joey is beyond me. I can't even go to the grocery store without his permission. I used to drop him off at work and take the car for the day. Now he takes the car and says there isn't anywhere I need to go. The only place I go is the library because we can walk there. So I'm all cooped up in the apartment and I feel so trapped. But I'm afraid to go out. What if he sees me?"

"Does he know you came to see me today?"

"Oh, my God, no! If he did know I wouldn't be here. This woman, Maria, I met at the library offered to drop me off here and take the kids to story hour. She's the one who gave me your card. I told her I had no way to get here and she brought me here to see you. She told me you helped her before. I didn't even think to ask her last name. That's how rude I've been lately. My mind is so full of fear, it's like I can't even have a normal conversation anymore. But I think she would bring me back again."

"O.K. But we're going to have to move fast. You are in danger and the sooner we can get you out of harm's way, the better. Here, take this literature about domestic violence and read it," Zoe said, handing the thick packet of papers over to Tina and pointing to certain parts as she showed it to her. "Here are the phone numbers for shelters, and don't hesitate to call them if you need to get out before our next session. And pay particular attention to the power and control wheel, here. It shows a pattern where the abuser builds up tension, explodes into violence, and then becomes loving again, begging for forgiveness and being 'sweet,' as you put it, only to return again to the beginning of the cycle. You'll see how his 'sweet' behavior is actually part of the battering cycle. The shelter will provide transportation if you need it, so call if you need to. I'm so glad you had the courage to come in today. Working together, we will bring you to safety."

"Thanks, and I'm sorry."

"What are you sorry for?"

"I don't know. I'm just sorry. I'm afraid you're mad at me."

"I am angry, but I'm not angry at you. I'm angry that your husband is hurting you. Nobody has the right to hurt you. Remember and hold on to that."

"OK. Thank you. Thank you for your help."

Tina turned to leave, still looking at the papers Zoe had given her. She almost walked into a well dressed young woman who was just getting herself seated in the waiting room. She thought the woman gave her a funny look but she wasn't sure. She quickly hid the information packet and scurried away to get into Maria's car.

CHAPTER 15

Diana and the Earthquake

"**W**hat's up?" Zoe said, as she took in Diana's tight body language and anxious facial expression.

"I had another weird dream last night," Diana said as she settled into Zoe's sofa.

"Tell me about it," Zoe said.

"First I was walking on this very hot and crowded street where there were stalls on the sidewalks. They were selling tee shirts, magic charms to keep you safe, and jewelry that they sold by the pound. People were speaking many different languages. I entered a wide area with stalls and push carts and there was an arched opening leading to a cave-like tunnel. There was a high, vaulted ceiling made of arches that were beautifully decorated like a cathedral. Everything was made of stone. It was dark in there but there were places where light was streaming down from the high, decorated ceiling, which looked very beautiful.

It was a big shopping area, but it was nothing like a mall. I was going up and down stairs on all different levels from one section of the marketplace to another. It was like a huge labyrinth with narrow passageways filled with what seemed like thousands of people. All of the stores had merchandise piled from floor to ceiling. Merchants were trying to sell me their wares by talking to me in many different languages. When I answered them in English, they spoke English to me. They invited me in to look at what they were selling and they asked me to come in and have some apple tea.

I stopped and asked this guy who was selling beautiful, intricately designed rugs, 'Where am I?' He said, 'In the Grand Bazaar.' In the dream, I thought he meant 'bizarre,' you know, like weird, but after I thought about it later, I realized he didn't. But I still didn't know where I was. So I asked another one of the merchants, 'Where are we?' and he didn't answer.

Then I saw a woman dressed all in black. She wore a black veil, which covered almost all of her face. Nothing was showing except her eyes. I went up to her and I begged her to tell me, 'Where am I? Where am I?' And she said, 'Istanbul.' I remember thinking to myself, 'behind that veil there's a lot she's not saying. She knows a lot, but she's not saying a lot.' So I asked her, "How did I get to Istanbul?" but she didn't answer me. I'm confused in the dream and everything was all jumbled in my mind. The lady dressed in black says, 'Soon it will be falling apart here. There are so many parts and pieces, what else could it do but fall apart? It's all going to collapse soon.' I woke up and had a horrible feeling something terrible was going to happen. But that was it. That's all I could remember of the dream." Diana began weeping softly. "It doesn't sound so terrible yet, does it?" she said, looking up at Zoe through her tear-filled eyes.

"I can see that it certainly felt terrible to you," Zoe cooed sympathetically.

Diana began crying harder, heaving big sighs, and gulping for air in between. "It was the news again; the same thing as before." She ripped several sheets of Kleenex out of the box, and wiped her eyes. "I didn't put on any eye make-up today because I knew I would just be crying it off in here. What's the point?" Diana attempted a wan smile as she searched Zoe's face, finding the caring and concern she had come to expect. Zoe sat patiently as Diana continued. "Three days passed and nothing happened, but I remembered the dream so vividly, it was like it really happened. I wasn't sure what it meant, but I knew I was going to come here and tell you about it. I couldn't stop thinking about that dream. I knew it had to mean something important."

"It sounds important," Zoe said softly, nodding her head as she looked into Diana's red and puffy face.

"And it was. It was the same thing again. The CNN thing again. Why does this keep happening to me? Why won't it leave me alone?" Diana grabbed another Kleenex and wiped her nose.

Zoe said nothing, while Diana continued sobbing, her voice getting higher and louder. "It was three days later and came on while I was doing the treadmill. The first story I heard when I did my walking was about this big earthquake in Turkey. I don't know very much about Turkey, but I had this terrible feeling that this was what the dream was about. So I went to look up Turkey in this big, giant atlas I have and that's when I saw that it was there."

"You saw it was there?"

"Istanbul."

"Hmmm," Zoe said.

"I went and got the encyclopedia and I looked up Turkey and it was there. Not the Grand Bizarre, like I thought, but the Grand Bazaar. It was in Istanbul, Turkey."

"What did that mean to you?" Zoe asked.

"What else could it mean, Zoe? It happened again. I dreamed about the earthquake days before it even happened. I had another premonition, another one of my visions. That's why I had such a scared feeling when I was in that marketplace. And I saw her, too. I saw her on TV. The lady dressed in black. They interviewed her. I really gasped when I saw that it was the woman from my dream. She was crying that her children and husband were killed in the earthquake. She was reaching out her arms and pleading up to heaven, as if she were asking God how he could do this to her. It was just like she said. It all fell apart and collapsed. It was like I could feel her pain. I felt like my children had died in that earthquake, or maybe even like I had died in that earthquake. That's how hard it hit me. She was in Istanbul, but not in the Grand Bazaar. It was further outside the main city, but that's where the earthquake was and they interviewed the lady in black. The black clothes were exactly the same as they were in the dream. I felt so sorry for her. I felt so sorry for all of them. There was nothing I could do. Nothing I could have done. Even if I had known where the earthquake was going to be and I had warned them. Even if I knew it was going to happen like the lady in the dream said. What could I have done? What could I have done to stop it? Nothing!"

"That's exactly right," Zoe said soothingly. "There was nothing you could have done to stop it."

"I know that. I know that in my head, but I feel like it's my fault those people died. Like I could have saved those people if only I could have understood the dream, but I didn't. I just went back to sleep, is what I did."

"When you had a dream about an earthquake, what else could you have done?"

"I didn't even know. I didn't know the lady was talking about an earthquake. I thought it was a dream about my therapy."

"That's interesting. Tell me more."

"Yeah, I thought that it was just symbolic. Like some of the dreams we talked about before. Like being in therapy is like being in a weird place where you don't know what's going on, and there is nothing but a lot of stuff there, all piled up, and you know you feel bad, and you are always afraid something even worse is going to happen. I thought it was maybe like I was afraid of falling apart and breaking into little pieces. Or even dying. I thought that was what the lady in black meant. You know, like black is the color you wear when someone dies, and how I was afraid that I was the one who was going to die when I saw the earthquake news?"

"That makes sense to me. Where do you think that fear might come from?" Zoe asked.

"From CNN."

"From CNN?" Zoe's eyebrow indicated her doubts about this.

"That's where I think my fear comes from. In fact, I know it. I know my fear comes from *CNN Headline News.*"

"How do you know that?"

"Because it's about real things that happen. When reality gets mixed up with nightmares, that's scary. I don't want all my dreams to happen in real life, but there's nothing I can do to stop them. When I watch *CNN Headline News* it just happens."

"So what do you make of that?"

"I think I should just stop watching *CNN Headline News*! I could do my treadmill listening to music instead."

"That might feel soothing to you." Zoe said.

"See, the trouble is the dreams. I can make myself think of other things when I'm awake, but the trouble is with the dreams because I can't control them. How can I make myself stop dreaming this stuff? I don't know how!"

"You're working on soothing yourself when you feel afraid." Zoe said, in her softest voice.

"See, what's hard is that I almost always feel afraid. That's why I have to keep myself busy. If I'm not busy I have too much time to think."

"And how is that working for you?" Zoe asked.

"It isn't."

"Avoiding the issues isn't working for you?" Zoe asked gently.

"I try to avoid them, but *CNN Headline News* gets in the way."

"Those headlines are filled with a lot of painful realities." Zoe said.

"Yeah, painful realities like little kids being murdered and smashed to smithereens in earthquakes. And I'm scared. I'm so scared I feel like a little kid myself sometimes."

"Hmmmm," Zoe said.

"But I'll tell you one thing I've learned here today," Diana said.

"What's that?" Zoe asked.

"I've learned that I have to stop watching *CNN Headline News*, because it's causing all my problems."

"*CNN Headline News* is causing all of your problems?"

"Yes."

"Is it causing all of your problems or is it reminding you of some of your problems?"

"I won't know until next week, after I try music instead of news."

"We can talk some more about it then," Zoe said.

Diana noticed Zoe leaning forward in her chair, a signal that the session was about to end. Diana felt panicky as she considered waiting another whole week to see Zoe again. Wordlessly, she got up and headed for the door. She grabbled hold of the doorknob and looked back at Zoe, but she felt like she just couldn't leave. There was something she needed to tell Zoe, something she was forgetting.

"Zoe! I almost forgot! It was her!"

"What was her?"

"The woman who had the appointment just before me today. I saw her leaving downstairs just before I came in. She was the one who was in danger in my other dream. I can feel it so strongly."

"Clients often have feelings about other people they see in the waiting room. If it still feels pressing to you next time, we talk about it some more then."

"Oh, O.K." Diana was holding her breath along with the door knob.

"I'll see you then," Zoe encouraged, and Diana turned and headed out the door, back into the real world.

CHAPTER 16

Rebecca, Leah and Zoe

"I just can't believe that they flunked me!" Rebecca cried when she got back home after her driver's test. "I only crashed into the curb once!" A mudslide of tears mixed with mascara had left raccoon circles around her eyes. Even Leah knew enough not to tease her.

"You can take the test again soon," Leah tried to soothe, but Rebecca was having none of it.

"Don't you dare go to school and tell anyone about this! I mean it! Promise me you won't tell anyone, Leah!"

"OK, OK, but I already told some of my friends you were taking it today. What should I say if they ask me if you got your license?"

"Tell them I'm dead!"

"No, really, Rebecca. What do you want me to tell our friends?"

"I'm not telling them anything because I'm not going to school. How could they do this to me?"

"Rebecca, it will be hard for you to tell your friends at school about this, but I can assure you that you are going to school," Zoe said firmly.

"Mom, no! Can't you just write me a note and say I'm sick? I can't go, Mom! Everybody will find out!"

"No, I cannot write you a note and say you are sick when you are not sick. You're going to school."

"Mom! I thought you were a therapist. I thought you were supposed to be sensitive to other people's feelings. What about my feelings? You don't even care!"

Zoe decided to ignore this. "I know you're very disappointed and embarrassed, 'Becca. But lots of people don't pass the test on the first try. I didn't when I took it, and I remember crying just like you're crying now. And I know Dad didn't pass it the first time he took it, either."

"Great! No wonder I flunked! It's genetic! What is the matter with this family? Why can't I come from a normal family?"

"What makes you think you don't come from a normal family?" Zoe asked.

"As if, Mom! Don't tell me you think this is a normal family! Dad is a computer geek who watches *Star Trek* re-runs and you work with crazy people. How normal is that?"

"Mom," Leah chimed in. "I know you want to think we're a normal family, but believe me, we're not. Yesterday when everyone was talking about *Take Your Daughter to Work Day*, I said, 'I wouldn't want to go to work with my mother! She works with people who are loony tunes.'"

"The people I work with are people who have problems they are courageous enough to face and to overcome. Some of them suffer with major mental illnesses, but that does not mean they are 'loony tunes.'"

"Mom, you've just gotten so used to being around crazy people that you think they are regular people. You don't even know what's normal anymore," Leah said. "But don't worry, Mom. It's not your fault. Don't feel bad about it or anything. It's just because your job is so weird."

"Hello! Is anybody listening to me?" Rebecca said, clearing her throat loudly. "Does anyone remember that I am the one who just ruined my reputation for life? I can't believe I didn't pass! I just can't believe it! How can I possibly go to school tomorrow? I told all of my friends I was taking it too."

"You can try again in a month or two, honey. Maybe you just need a little more practice," Zoe said in her most soothing tones.

"A month or two! I'll be the only one left in my class who isn't driving yet. It's so humiliating! I hope no one saw me in our car! It's no wonder I flunked the test, because our car is so old! We shouldn't even call it a car, we should call it a carcass!"

Everyone was silent, holding her breath, when Leah started to giggle and Zoe could not suppress her own laughter, either. Before long, Rebecca was joining in, and the laughter released all the pent-up tension of a difficult afternoon.

"That's what we're going to call it from now on! The Carcass! I can't wait to tell Dad when he gets home from work. I know he'll think that's funny. Whenever he drives us to school we tease him about how old the car is. I keep telling him he should get himself a new one so that I can have his old one. Do you think Dad could take me out to practice some more this weekend, Mom? No offense, but you're such a nervous wreck when I'm driving that you make me even more nervous, and I think he's a better teacher."

"No, I agree. I do get too anxious with it. Well, of course you'll have to ask him, but my guess is that he will be able to squeeze that in this weekend."

The phone rang and both of the girls ran to get it. Rebecca handed the phone to Zoe, her eyebrows dropping in disappointment. "It's for you, Mom. It's Jessica."

"Thanks, honey. I'll get it upstairs."

"Jessie, hi. We just got back from going to Rebecca's driver's test."

"Oh, my God! She has her license already?"

"No. Actually, she didn't pass the test, but please make sure you don't mention that to Stephen. She is feeling humiliated because she told all her friends she was taking the test and now she's going to have to tell them all that she didn't pass."

"Oh, that must be tough for her."

"Yes, it was completely fraught with adolescent angst. But it was also hilarious for me. Rebecca gave me marching orders prior to the test and told me I HAD to remember to put on my seat belt because her friend's mother hadn't put on her seat belt and her friend flunked the test when she didn't tell her mother to buckle up. Rebecca also told me that I was going to have to go out on the test with her. That surprised me because they don't do it that way in California, or at least they didn't when I was a kid."

"Many eons ago."

"Yes. Anyway, I cleaned out the back of the car, which is always so disgusting that Daniel calls it a 'Major Land-Fill Project' with all the crap the kids throw on the floor."

Jessica laughed. "We call our backseat the Big Dig, and it's not getting done any faster than Boston is!"

"So anyway, I clean out the back of the car, but I only clean one side of it, behind the passenger seat. When the examiner gets in the car he tells me I have to sit behind the driver's side. So as quickly as I can, I try to shove all of the garbage over to the other side, but obviously I missed something important."

"Why, what happened?"

"I go to fasten the seat belt and I feel something cold and gooey. No matter how much I try to push the thing in, it won't go in. So I pull out my hand, and it's covered with dark goo, which I finally decide is chocolate pudding."

"Chocolate pudding!" Jessica laughed.

"Somehow, I've managed to sit on a snack pack of chocolate pudding that the kids have left in the back seat and I am covered with pudding all over my backside. Naturally, I'm trying to hide this from the examiner, so he doesn't flunk 'Becca. So here I am all during the test, trying to hold the seat belt in place so the guy won't see it isn't buckled. Picture me with my hand full of goo, trying to look completely nonchalant, and trying not to laugh. We go out with me still holding the seat belt in the chocolate pudding, and we don't go more than two blocks when Rebecca crashes the car into the curb. The examiner tells her to return to the registry and the test ends."

"Oh my God! Was anybody hurt when she crashed into the curb?"

"No, no one was hurt, but naturally, that is an automatic flunk. So Rebecca is crying, and I'm trying to console her, and clean off my derriere at the same time. I'm pulling Wet Ones baby wipes out of the glove compartment and trying to clean up enough so that I don't bring the chocolate pudding with me into the driver's seat. So here I am, standing in the parking lot at the Registry, trying to clean a big brown stain off my ass while Rebecca is crying about how embarrassed SHE is!"

Jessica was laughing and making a whooping sound whenever she inhaled. "Stop! My stomach hurts! I've got to get some air!"

"Never a dull moment in life with these kids! I get home and I use every kind of spoon I can think of to try to scoop the chocolate pudding out of the seat belt mechanism, but none of them worked. So finally, I am in the back seat of the car with a turkey baster trying to suck out all the pudding to the sound of Rebecca's wails and turkey-baster pudding farts."

Jessica was still whooping and fighting for air, "Stop, I can't breathe!"

Zoe pressed on, undaunted. "I couldn't get the turkey baster in deep enough, so I changed my tactics. I cleaned out the turkey baster, no small task in itself, and filled it with water, using it to squirt water into the seat belt latch. Then I had a river of water mixed with chocolate pudding, which I sopped up with rolls and rolls of paper towels. Now the whole car smells like chocolate pudding. Somehow, I get the damned thing to latch again, but I have no idea if the seat belt mechanism will ever work again or if it is permanently gummed up. So I throw all my wet, pudding-stained clothes into the washer, grab a robe, throw some chicken and potatoes into the oven, and collapse in my recliner to watch the news."

"It sounds like a nightmare!" Jessica chuckled.

"Meanwhile, Rebecca has been crying, 'I'm ruined! My life is ruined! How can they do this to me! I only crashed into the curb once!'"

"So here's the question. What do we name this one?"

"How about *The Great Chocolate Pudding Disaster*?"

"Or *I Fought the Curb and the Curb Won*."

"How about *I Dream of Zoe with the Light Brown Bum*?"

"I think I vote for *The Great Chocolate Pudding Disaster*."

"Yes, it has a nice ring to it."

"Can you stand it?"

"Well, I've been standing it, so I guess I can stand it some more. You and Anna are the ones who are just getting started all over again. So how is the little one?"

"Little."

"Sounds good to me!" Zoe said, looking wistful.

"The news I called to tell you might cheer Rebecca up. I think our two are headed for a full-blown romance. Stephen wants to take 'Becca to a dance at his school. He's been trying to work up the nerve to call her and ask her to go with him, but of course, you're not supposed to know that."

"Really? Well, I can tell you on my end that Rebecca would probably be thrilled about it."

"That's what I was hoping you'd say. Here, I'll put him on the phone and they can talk. He asked me to call you and ask you first if she would want to go out with him before he asked her directly."

"O.K. I'll say goodbye now, then."

"O.K. I'll see you at the office tomorrow."

"Hello, Stephen? Let me go get Rebecca for you." Zoe went downstairs to get her daughter. "Becca? Stephen wants to talk to you."

Rebecca gasped. "You didn't tell him I was going to take my driver's test, did you?"

"No, honey. I was talking to his mother. I didn't tell him anything."

Rebecca took the phone in her bedroom and came out within a few minutes. Her tears were gone and she was beaming. "Stephen asked me out. I'm going to a dance with him at his school! This is so totally wickedly awesome!"

Leah began bouncing up and down on the couch. "I could tell he liked you! I saw him looking at you at the pool party. And he wasn't just looking at you. He was 'looking at you' looking at you! Do you like him?"

"Yes, I already told you I like him."

"Yes, but what I mean is do you 'like him' like him or do you just like him?"

"I 'like him' like him."

"I 'like him' like him, too."

"Well, too bad! He obviously doesn't like you! He likes me! You're too young for him, anyway. Don't even think about talking to him. Mom, tell her not to flirt with him!"

"I think she understands that would be inappropriate."

"Are you going to kiss him?" Leah asked, her blue eyes growing rounder as she pursed her lips.

"That's none of your business," Rebecca said.

"C'mon. Tell me. Are you going to kiss him?" Leah asked. "Inquiring minds want to know!"

"Inquiring minds better mind their own business! Mom, tell her to shut up!"

"Leah, please remember to give your sister enough respect that you don't violate her privacy."

"Violate her privacy! God, Mom! Don't make it sound like I'm a rapist or something! I just asked her a simple question. If she doesn't want to answer it, she can just say no. Why do you always take her side?"

"She doesn't always take my side! She always takes your side!" Rebecca protested.

"She does not! How can you say that! Mom's always on your side and I always get into trouble for doing nothing, all because of you!"

"My inquiring mind has a question, too," Zoe said. "Are you two ever going to stop bickering?"

"No, I don't think so," said Leah, thoughtfully.

"I think she's right," said Rebecca. "We could tell you we're gonna stop, but realistically, we probably never will."

"Wonderful! At last we have some agreement!" Zoe exclaimed. "Let's just leave it at that."

CHAPTER 17

Tina, Joe and the Parakeet

*J*oe held the cigarette lighter in one hand and the parakeet in the other. Tina's eyes widened and she fingered the business card in her pocket as she saw her husband squeezing her pretty blue bird.

"You filthy slut! The grocery store, huh? Is that where you went? You expect me to believe that? Who in the hell sent you these flowers?" Joe flicked the lighter and moved the bird closer to the flame. "How can you lie to me in front of your own son? Joey, tell me, where did Mama go today? Tell Daddy where Mama went and then I won't hurt the birdie."

Joey's eyes widened. "Price Chopper. Mama and me get to go to Price Chopper and Mama let me ride the horsie. Don't hurt the birdie, Daddy."

"Price Chopper, huh? Well, where else did you and Mama go?"

"Story Hour at the library. Rico was there too."

"Rico! Tell me, Joey, who is Rico?"

"My friend."

"And who was Mama's friend today? Who was with Mama today when you went to story hour at the library?"

"Me! Mama was with me! And Rico was with his Mommy, too. We readed a story about a choo-choo train. Rico is from my school, Daddy."

"That's right. I remember you telling me about Rico. And where did Mama get the flowers, Joey?" Joey looked confused and worried.

"Joe, please, you're scaring him!" Tina protested.

"Mama get the flowers at Price Chopper. Mama likes pretty flowers and I like pretty flowers, too."

"That's OK, Joey. But that's not real good. Flowers are for girls, Joey. Men like us don't like flowers. Now because you were such a good boy today, Daddy won't have to clip the birdie's wings." Joe let go of the parakeet and it quickly flew back to its perch inside the cage. "Now go watch some cartoons, Joey. Mama and I have to talk." Joey looked at his father anxiously, worried that the screaming would start again.

Joe was careful to make sure Joey was out of earshot so he wouldn't have to hear what a worthless whore his mother was. "Tina, I swear to God I will kill you and that bird if I ever catch you with another man. Did you teach Joey to use the grocery store as an alibi? How does a three-year-old boy come up with an alibi like that on his own?" The muscles on Joe's jaw were tensing as he clenched his teeth in rage.

"He couldn't. He's just telling the truth about where we went and what we did." Tina began to tremble as if her body remembered what was coming next even though her mind was numbed to it.

"You expect me to believe that you didn't tell him to say that? How long have you been lying to me, bitch? I know you are sneaking around in some way. I can smell it. THERE WILL BE NO SNEAKING AROUND OUT OF THIS HOUSE! Is that understood?" Tina cast her eyes downward and shook her head even more than the rest of her was shaking. Joey came back into the room and clutched his mother's legs, so Joe lowered his voice again. "You will go where I tell you to go and do what I tell you to do."

"Sure, Joe. I only went to the grocery store so I could get food for us and I took Joey to the library because I know you want your son to grow up to be a smart man."

"Alright then. But I don't want you wasting any more of my hard earned money on flowers! They only rot the next day anyway. What is the matter with you? Are you trying to turn my son into a pansy? Do you need to have your fat ass whipped to stop spending my money on rotting garbage? Who needs a whipping, Joey? Do you need a whipping, or does Mommy need a whipping?"

"Mommy!" Joey moved behind his mother's legs.

Tina could feel the panic rising along with her stomach contents. *I can't throw up! He'll beat me even more if I throw up.* Tina began gasping as she remembered how Joe had shoved her head into the toilet and flushed it repeatedly as he held her down by the back of her neck the last time she had vomited. She'd almost drowned. She tried to will her stomach contents to settle down.

"Look at your son, Tina! He's hiding behind you like a sorry ass sissy. You're turning my son into a panty waist."

"He gets scared when he hears you hollering, Joe. He's just a baby."

"No son of mine is a baby! He's three years old, for Christ's sake, and you still have him in diapers. Maybe he'd stop peeing himself all the time if you stopped putting him in diapers. Joey, are you a baby or a big boy?"

"I'm a big boy, Daddy!"

"That's my boy!" Joe scooped little Joey into his arms. Now, come into the bathroom with me and I'll show you how a man pees. No wonder you don't know how to be a man when you're around women all day."

"OK, Joe, I'll go finish dinner for you while you help little Joey. I know you've been upset since your mom died. You don't really want to be angry like this, do you?"

"I wouldn't have to be so angry if it weren't for you. I swear to God, I almost had to hurt you in front of Joey, my own son, and all because you are a sneaky slut spending the grocery money on flowers. I better not come home and find anymore Goddamned flowers! What do you think this is, a funeral parlor? Haven't we had enough fucking funerals in this family?"

"I'm sorry Joe. I think the flowers reminded you of your Mom's funeral. I'm sorry." Joe briefly had tears well up in his eyes, before he hardened again.

"Who do you think will be in the coffin the next time there's a funeral, bitch?" Joe reached out and grabbed Tina by her hair and she winced as he pulled it tighter and tighter. "I'll give you a hint. It won't be me and it won't be Joey. Because next time it will be your wings I'll burn. You need your wings singed, don't you? Maybe we won't even need a coffin. We could just have a cremation." Tina felt as if she could barely breathe as she saw Joe flick his lighter again and bring it closer and closer to her shiny black hair.

"Joe, please. You're hurting me. I promise I'll be good. I won't get any more flowers if you don't want me to. I didn't know you didn't want me to. I wanted to make the table look pretty for your dinner, that's all, Joe, honest. Now let me go finish the dinner, Joe, so I can serve you a nice meal. Don't you deserve a nice meal after a hard day at work? You'll feel better after you eat."

"Then get the hell into that kitchen and bring me another beer, if you know what's good for you."

Tina moved quickly enough to escape another beating this time. *How much more of this can I take?* Joe seemed to be threatening to kill her more and more often recently. Her time was spent trying to think up an escape plan that would work. She had no money and no access to money. Joe took care of that. *Joe will kill me if I try to leave him. And then what would happen to Joey?* Tina's mind wandered around in the same circles they always did; how to protect Joey, escape Joe, and still remain alive. If she failed, Joey would be left alone with Joe.

Tina wondered how she came to be caught by the shambles that was her life. Just last week, after she saw Zoe there was that horrible fight that Joe started over some burnt toast. But then Joe was so apologetic afterwards, so sweet and vulnerable. He showered her with kisses, told her he could never forgive himself if he ever hurt her again, begged for her forgiveness. It was really only since his mom died that he had become a monster instead of a man. Tina thought of a Richard Pryor comedy routine about the movie *The Amityville Horror* that she had seen on TV, years ago. "What's the matter with these white people? Don't they know enough to get out the house?" Richard had asked, or no, maybe it was Eddie Murphy. Tina didn't remember anymore. *Good advice, Mr. Comedian. Amityville couldn't be any worse than this.*

Tina wanted so badly to find somewhere where she could once again feel safe. *If only Mom and Dad were still alive. They would help me.* She reached into her pocket and pulled the well-worn card out. *Zoe Wentworth, MSW, LICSW, Psychotherapist. Is it possible that Zoe could actually help me escape? But how could I get there again without Joe finding out, and how could I pay for it without accounting for every cent of the money to Joe? How many times can I impose on Maria to drive me there? And what if Joe finds out?* Tina continued cooking dinner as if her life depended on it, only breaking her reverie when Joe began shouting again.

"How long does it take, lard ass? Get a move on!"

Tina raced to bring him the beer, knowing it would only fuel his temper. *How long does it take?*

CHAPTER 18

Zoe, Jessica and Dreams

Zoe and Jessica were driving home from Boston after attending a clinical training at Boston University about using dreams with clients.

"What did you think of the seminar?" Jessica asked.

"I loved it! What did you think?"

"Well, you know me. I'm not much for this woo-woo stuff. Clients seldom present their dreams to me, anyway, so I'm not sure I'll be able to use much of it. But it was okay, I guess. We got Continuing Education Units for it, and it wasn't too painful."

"That's funny. I found it so useful and so pertinent. I am still struggling with that client I told you about who seems to be having psychic dreams about my other clients. Remember when we broke into smaller groups and presented cases about client dreams?"

"Yes."

"Well, I got a chance to talk to some of the other therapists about my client and about their experiences with their patient's dreams. Some of the clinicians feel like there is an uncanny way that clients have of zeroing in on material that is very current with the therapist's own issues. For instance, one of the clinicians was saying that the very week that her daughter left for college that several clients were telling her dreams about college, about leaving, about mothers and daughters saying good-bye, about loss, about adolescent girls."

"That's probably just the therapist projecting her own stuff onto her clients. She is just hearing selectively."

"Perhaps. But a number of them have had experiences where clients told them something that they couldn't possibly know about."

"Like what?"

"Well, one woman said that she needed to cancel a client appointment because her son had broken his arm at school. She said that when she called this client to cancel the appointment that the client told her that she knew she was going to cancel that day because she had a dream that the therapist's son had fallen out of a tree and broken his arm."

"Had he fallen out of a tree and broken his arm?"

"No, he had broken his leg playing Lacrosse at school. But still. It's pretty weird, isn't it? The patient had never even been told that the therapist had a son, and she came up with a son and a broken limb on the very day that it happened. Everyone seemed to have a story about that kind of thing."

"And that's all they are, Zoe—stories. You need be careful. It sounds to me like you're getting caught up in your client's delusional system. How are you going to help her if you lose your own reality testing? If your client is having these dreams she needs you to reassure her that they are nothing more than dreams."

"Then how do you explain the earthquake dream?"

"What earthquake dream?"

"She told me she had a dream about the earthquake in Turkey before it happened, too."

"Did she tell you this before the earthquake happened?"

"No. She told me this after it happened, but she said that she dreamed it before it happened."

"Zoe! This is just classic resistance. She's entertaining you with dramatic stories instead of doing her work. Ask yourself what issue she was avoiding while she was telling you about this. She's making up these far-fetched stories about super powers and premonitions and you believe her. Are you hearing yourself?"

"I'm not saying I am believing everything she says. She told me that *CNN Headline News* is causing all of her problems."

"When a client tells you that all of her problems come from the TV set you should be thinking psychotic, not psychic!"

"I know. I know. But I just don't see her as psychotic. I don't know what to think. It just keeps happening. You know, that's funny. That's what she said to me during her first session with me. 'It just keeps happening.' Maybe you're right. Maybe I am getting pulled into her delusional system," Zoe said, doubtfully.

"Try to make sure that you don't join her there, because joining with her on this delusion won't accomplish what you want. I don't think you can pull her out of it by going in there with her. You need to be reality's ally in this. Your instincts are usually good about these things, Zoe. Trust your gut. But just don't get so joined with her on this delusion that you don't see it for what it is."

"You're right, I guess. And I appreciate your input about it. Thanks, Jess."

CHAPTER 19

Tina, Zoe and Fear

Tina sank into Zoe's sofa and began crying, her petite body wracked with desperate, choking sobs. "It's real fire now. He's stopped threatening with the lighter and he's started lighting fires all over," Tina said, with her voice cracking as she looked pleadingly up at Zoe.

"Fires?" Zoe asked in alarm.

"He's setting fires. He's burning candles, all over the house, and he's playing with the flames." Zoe's brow furrowed as she mimicked Tina's anxiety-stricken countenance. "I'm so scared! I keep getting diarrhea and running to the bathroom, my only place to get away from him. I'm even scared after I lock myself in the bathroom, afraid he'll break the door down. I keep flushing the toilet over and over again so he won't beat me for stinking up the house. Then I'm afraid that he'll beat me for flushing the toilet too many times and wasting water. I never know what to do and I can't even think straight. I never know what's going to set him off again."

Zoe stiffened as she sat up taller in her chair and almost imperceptibly moved closer to Tina.

"Yesterday the only thing that stopped me from soiling my pants was this terror that he would actually kill me if I did. I don't know what I'm going to do. What if I can't hold it in anymore? I can't believe what's happening in my life. How sad is it that he's actually scaring the shit out of me?"

Zoe's facial expression mirrored the acute, intense fear she felt on behalf of her terrorized client.

"His talk is getting crazier, too. He's talking about 'burnt offerings' and 'sacrificial lambs,' and he's set up an altar."

"An altar?"

"Yes. He has all these pictures set up of his mother and the Blessed Virgin surrounded by candles. He won't let anyone come near it. When he isn't setting up more fires he's saying these crazy things and looking up like he's talking to someone. He talks like somebody is talking back to him, like he's on the phone or something. But then I look to see who he's talking to and no one else is even there."

"This sounds very disturbing to me. I'm afraid for you and for Joey."

"That makes two of us! I want to leave, but Zoe, honest to God, I know he'll hunt me down to the far corners of the earth if he has to. How can I get away? When I look in his eyes I feel like I am looking into pure evil. His eyes are glazed over like he isn't even there or something. Like some kind of fiendish zombie. It's like he isn't the man I married anymore. It's more like I'm living with a demon who has possessed him." The pitch of Tina's voice got higher and higher as she spoke until her voice sounded nearly hysterical.

"You sound terrified, as well you should be. I hear that you're afraid for your life."

"I'm beyond terrified. I'm scared shitless and then I'm afraid about that too." Tina's voice swooped into high-pitched unnatural laughter.

"Is anything getting in the way of your making an escape plan? I think our number one priority here has to be to get you to a safe place."

"Is there such a thing as a safe place? I can hardly even remember what it feels like to feel safe." Tina's whole frame shook from her desperate, renewed convulsions of sobbing. "What if he burns down the house when Joey and I are asleep? I don't even think I'd really care anymore for my own sake. At least death would be an escape. But what if he kills Joey? He's obsessed with this new death kick now."

"This is very troubling and serious severe pathology that you're describing to me. Fire setting behaviors are a clear sign that he is out of control. I'm afraid for Joey and you. You need to get to safety."

"And believe it or not, there's more I haven't told you. I heard this pounding and pounding one night that woke me up. I couldn't imagine what it was, so I got out of bed to go see. He was right in the living room building something out of wood. I saw a hammer in his hand and every time I think of him now all I can see is that hammer. He was making a big wooden box but I couldn't tell what it was. I got back in bed before he could see that I was awake and start something. When I got up in the morning I saw what it was." Tina stopped there as if she were suspended in time while Zoe waited patiently.

"It's hard to say these things aloud. It's painful and difficult for you. And you need to act fast now, which is also hard," Zoe encouraged.

Tina gulped and continued. "When I got out of bed in the morning I saw that he had a coffin set up in the living room, surrounded by candles. It looked like the funeral home when his mother died. I kept thinking, 'Who is this coffin for?' and I was afraid of the answer."

"You're afraid because you know the risks of what you have to do."

"I know I have to leave him now, but I'm just so scared." Tina's petite body shook with profound sobs. Her voice shrieked like a smoke detector. "He'll find us wherever we go. He's going to kill us, I know it."

"Are you ready to go to a safe place?" Zoe asked gently.

"It doesn't feel like there is a safe place," Tina wailed.

"You're not able to envision that now."

"How would I even get there?"

Zoe thought of the 11:00 a.m. and 1:00 p.m. cancellations she had heard on her voice mail that morning. It would take a little more than an hour each way, but with her noon time slot free for lunch she realized she could make it in time to be back for her 2:00 p.m. client. *It's completely contrary to my clinical training to drive a client some-where to rescue them, but a Higher Power is telling me that I not only have to get her to a shelter myself, but I have to get her farther away from here than the local protective services. This isn't only about wife beating, my gut tells me he is planning to kill her, so this is a matter of life and death. Besides, if she moves out of state then she will no longer be my client, so I think a boundary violation would be justified here.* "Where is Joey right now?"

"He's with Maria, the friend who dropped me off. She has both of the kids at the library for Story Hour."

"And Joe? Where is he?"

"At work," Tina said, still shaking.

"Good. I don't have an appointment after this for another few hours. I can take you and your son to a safe place."

"But I don't even have any clothes. I have nothing for Joey. How could I do that?"

"I'm going to take you to safety. When you get there, everything you need will be taken care of."

"But how?"

"You'll see when you get there. The less you know the better, for your own safety. All you need now is willingness. Are you willing to go with me now?"

"I'm afraid."

"I know. You've been afraid for a very long time," Zoe said while Tina sniffed, snuffled and wiped her eyes with tissues.

"Are you more afraid to come with me to safety or to return to your home, your violent husband, fire, and a coffin?"

"I know it sounds crazy but I'm actually more afraid to go with you. He'll kill me if he finds out where I am."

"I don't doubt that. But I also don't doubt that you need to get your child and yourself to safety. There is an opportunity for that now. He can't possibly have any idea of the plan because we didn't know about it until you got here. I think it would be difficult to have any better opportunity than this in the future, because after this you would know about it and may accidentally say something that would give yourself away."

"I don't know. I'm so scared it's like I'm numb. I feel like I'm already dead. Like I'm frozen and I can't even move."

"It feels to you like your fear is paralyzing you, just like it was when you first came to me for help. Despite that fear, you did come to me for help. It felt to you like you couldn't move because of the fear, but the reality is that you did move despite the fear. Then you were afraid to come back, but somehow you did. Do you think you would be able to do again what you've already done successfully in the past?"

"When you put it like that I think maybe I could because I was afraid to come to you the first time and he hasn't found out about that. And I was also afraid to come back today, but I did it."

"That's exactly right. You have the power to help your son and yourself to safety. Are you willing to allow me to help you?"

"Right now? I need my stuff. I'm not going to have any money and I need clothes for me and Joey. I don't think I can do it without our stuff."

"Yes. Right now. Now is the best opportunity."

"I was afraid before and that worked out O.K." Tina scraped her upper lip with her teeth and worry furrowed her brow. "I just couldn't believe it when I read that power and control wheel you gave me. It was like the story of my life. I always thought that Joe wasn't really like the other wife-beaters because he could be so sweet sometimes. But then I saw the pattern described in the pamphlet, tension mounting until the abuse happens, and then a release in tension, followed by the man bringing gifts to the woman, begging for forgiveness. Then tension mounts again and around it goes. I always thought he wasn't like the others, because he always said he was sorry afterwards, but he fit that pattern exactly.

"You're right. When Joe is sweet and apologetic afterwards that is also part of the abuse cycle. You can take Joey back to your crazy, violent husband or you can bring him to safety. It's completely your choice."

Tina thought Zoe's face looked just like the face on the statue of the Madonna at church. *It's a sign from the Blessed Virgin.* "O.K. I'll go, but only because you're going with me. I'm too scared to go alone. Are you sure you're not too busy?"

"Yes, I am busy. I am busy helping you. I can't imagine that anything else I do today will be as important as getting you to safety." Tina relaxed visibly at this. All of the phone calls went quickly and smoothly and Zoe was pleased to see that Tina was writing a list of all of the things she needed to pack while Zoe was on the phone.

"You said you needed some things from your apartment?" Zoe asked.

"Yes, but I'm afraid to go back there. I'm afraid I won't be able to leave again."

"We still have another half hour before your friend would come by after the session."

"Yes, it's early enough that Story Hour is probably still going on."

"Great. Then if we pick up Joey at the library first, we could go to your apartment briefly, and still make it in time for you to get to safety and for me to get back in time for my next client. I can wait in the car with Joey while you go upstairs and get your things."

"What if Joe is there?"

"How likely is that?"

"Not really very likely. He doesn't get off work until five."

"Does he ever come home early?"

"No."

"O.K., then."

"O.K." They got into Zoe's car and headed for the library. Tina rushed in to get Joey.

"I thought you needed me to pick you up at Zoe's office. How did you get here?" Maria asked.

"I got a ride. Maria, I'm sorry but I don't have any time to explain now. Thanks. Thank you so much for everything! I gotta run!"

"Mommy, I want to hear the rest of the story!" Joey protested, tugging on his mother's sleeve.

"I know you do, Honey Bear, but we're in a big hurry now, so I will read you another story later. We have to go now."

"NOOOO!" Joey's loud wails only made Tina rush more quickly to get him out of the library and into Zoe's car. Once the car started to move he quickly settled down.

Zoe, Tina and Joey quickly arrived at Tina's Lincoln Street apartment. As Tina took a deep breath, and pushed open the door to let herself in, she was assaulted with the smell of stale smoke and candle wax. She began to pack by hastily throwing everything she and Joey needed into a large denim laundry bag. Suddenly, she heard noises. She jumped, startled, and gasped, holding her breath, afraid that Joe was home. When she turned to look she was relieved to find that it was just the parakeet moving around in his cage. She shuddered when she heard loud squawk from the parakeet, remembering the image of Joe and the cigarette lighter. Glancing around furtively, Tina quietly packed up enough of Joey's belongings and her own that she and her son would be able to make do. She locked up, returned to the car, and they headed down Interstate 495.

"I don't know how I can thank you enough for helping me," Tina said to Zoe, her eyes filling with tears.

"You reward me with the gift of your trust by showing remarkable courage in accepting my help," Zoe said quietly.

Tina felt so moved by Zoe's words that she was silent. She held her breath, unsure if it was really safe to let go and relax. *Breathe. It's okay. I can breathe now. We're safe. He doesn't know where we are.* But her teeth were chattering and she was trembling.

Zoe took Tina and Joey to the main office of the women's protective shelter in Providence, Rhode Island. Zoe knew of this shelter, which accepted children as well as their mothers, through a friend and colleague who worked in Rhode Island. Tina knew there was no way that Joe could possibly know where she was, but she was terrified thinking of what he would do when he came home and found out she and Joey were gone. *Is this really going to work? Oh, my God, what if he finds us?* She was used to planning every move all day based on anticipating Joe's reaction and trying to avert his wrath.

Zoe didn't know the location of the safe house, but she had no trouble finding the central office in Providence, and she walked with Tina into the office. "O.K., Tina. This is it," Zoe said, lightly touching Tina's arm. "I have to hurry back for my next client. The staff will help you from here. Take good care."

Tina felt panic when she realized Zoe was leaving, but a middle-aged African-American woman, stepped up and took over.

"I'm Sondra," she said warmly. "And who is this little one?"

"That's Joey," Tina said, barely able to speak.

"Well, hello, Joey? How are you?"

"Good."

"And how old are you?" Sondra asked, without getting an answer. "How would you like to play with these toys while I talk with your Mama?"

Joey went right up to a bright yellow truck and began moving it over the floor, saying, "Vroom! Vroom!"

Sondra explained how the program worked and told Tina what to expect, while Joey played. Then Sondra asked Tina and Joey to get in the back of a station wagon with smoked glass windows. "We don't take chances here. Safety is always number one." Sondra gave Tina a beautiful broad smile, her straight white teeth gleaming next to her rich dark brown skin. Sondra was so helpful that Tina was almost able to believe that she and Joey would be safe, as she looked out the window on the way to the safe house. They drove to a large but shabby Victorian home in a residential neighborhood. The house showed no outward sign of being any different than any other house on the quiet, tree-lined street.

How can all these strangers be so kind when my own husband is so cruel? Tina felt bewildered and overwhelmed by how quickly her entire life was changing, and she held on to Joey's hand more tightly than usual. Tina bounced lightly on the bed in her new room, relief just beginning to loosen the grip of fear. *This is like a dream come true.* But dreams were only owned by the sunlight. That night, terrifying nightmares filled the long, dark hours with incessant pursuit by the monster who was her husband. She awakened to the image of Joe reaching out to strangle her, his hands tightening around her neck until her voice was silenced and she was unable to scream. *Will I ever be able to fall asleep without fear and wake up without nightmares again?*

CHAPTER 20

Zoe, Diana and Tina

Diana wasted no time in pouring out a flood of words that had been dammed up inside of her, while Zoe listened carefully, trying not to be swept away. "Remember when I told you about a dream I had at our last session?"

"Yes, as I recall we had planned to discuss that some more today. You were saying that you had some very strong feelings about another client whom you saw here in the waiting room. You brought this up just as you were leaving."

"Yeah. When I saw her I just couldn't believe it! I mean, there she was! It was totally unbelievable."

"Hmmm. It sounds like you had some very strong feelings."

"Well, yeah, but it's not just about my feelings! It's about what's going to happen."

"Let's explore some of those feelings."

Diana rolled her eyes and looked straight up as if she were seeking answers on the ceiling. "God, this is so frustrating! I can't get anyone to understand! She's in danger, OK? Do you get it? I don't know who she is, but I do know she's in danger. You've got to help her!"

Zoe sat in silence for a moment before she offered an interpretation to Diana. "Sometimes when we have very strong and overpowering feelings they are simply too difficult for us to hold on to. It's very uncomfortable to have feelings that are so strong that they're hard to contain. Sometimes, the way we can cope with this is to project those feelings onto other people. This is usually an unconscious process. It's kind of like using the other person to hold the feelings we have that we're unable to own. It's called projection."

"O.K. I get that. It's kind of like using the other person as a movie screen and the person who is having the feelings is the projector putting the feelings on the screen." Diana said, impatiently.

"Yes. Like a movie projector. Exactly. Keeping this in mind, let's consider your feelings about being in danger," Zoe said.

"Do you mean that if I'm doing this whole movie projector thing, then it could be me who is feeling like I'm in danger?" Diana asked doubtfully.

"Yes. My guess is that something is feeling dangerous to you here."

"Well, something IS feeling dangerous to me. But I don't care about myself. I only care about the other woman from the waiting room. She's the one you have to help. It's a matter of life and death!"

"I'm hearing how urgent this feels to you."

Diana felt exhausted after a week of chewing on anxiety like stale gum. "Listen. I get what you're saying about this projecting thing, but I'm telling you this really doesn't seem like it's about me. You've got to believe me! It's about that other woman in the waiting room. I keep seeing fire around her. She's surrounded by candles, but not just a few candles. I keep seeing a whole shit pile of candles. I see her in a coffin with candles all around her. I feel like if I don't warn her, this man is going to kill her. Maybe she's in some weird religious cult or something, because this man who is there with her is like a devil."

Zoe almost gasped but she managed to contain her shock and surprise. *My God! She's talking about Joe! How could she have known? I wonder if she put her head against the door and listened in on the session I had with Tina last time? How could I ask her without accusing her and without breaching Tina's confidentiality?* "Let's talk a little bit about the sequence of events and see if we can detect any patterns," Zoe said in calm, soothing tones, despite the alarms ringing inside her head. "You told me about the dream you had right at the very end of the session. Do you remember?"

"Yes! That's what I'm saying! I told you about the dream and then I went out into your waiting room and she was there!"

"Who was there?"

"The woman who is the main character from my dream. The mother of the little boy I was in the other dream. I mean, there she was, right in front of me. She's in so much danger! She's being abused by this psycho Satanic man who is going to kill her. Near the end of the dream she was dead in the coffin, and she was this ghastly ashen gray color. Then all of a sudden she opened her eyes, sat up and reached up her arms to me and said, 'Help me!' It was totally horrible how she came back from the dead and everything. That's what I've been trying to tell you. That woman in your waiting room who came right before me the week before last, she was the person I dreamed about. She was the woman in a coffin on top of a funeral pyre surrounded by hundreds of candles."

"I see. And after you felt like you recognized her, what then?"

"I practically ran to the car. My heart was pounding so fast and I felt like I couldn't catch my breath. It was like whatever was happening to her was contagious or something. I realized I had to get away from it, like I was going to drown in it or something. I don't want to have these movie projector feelings. It's scaring the holy shit out of me! I just wanted to get away and get back to the office and talk to Roz about it."

"So immediately after the session, you quickly left my office to return to work," Zoe's mind was spinning like a spirograph. *How in the hell could she have known about Tina and Joe?*

"Yes. But of course I wasn't in any shape to get any work done or anything. Thank God Rozzie was able to calm me down."

"Roz helped you to calm yourself when you got back to the office." Zoe said, stalling for time as she struggled to make sense of what she was hearing.

"Yes. Roz told me that I know I'm psychic and I should just accept it. She said I shouldn't be so afraid of it because it's actually useful. She reminded me that it's helped me to make placements because I always get this funny feeling whenever my client companies have job openings, and when I call, I find out my hunch was right. She said I shouldn't get so shook up about it because lots of people are psychic and almost everyone has hunches about things. Roz thinks the problem is just that I'm such a nice person that I want to help other people all the time. But she said that I really can't help other people all the time because a million bad things happen to other people every day. If I keep trying to save them because I'm getting messages about it, I could wind up spending my whole life trying to rescue people I don't even know. Roz said I should think about my own life too."

"And how did you feel about that?"

"I felt good. I mean, she is right. Catastrophes are everywhere all the time if you think about it."

"It sounds like something is feeling dangerous and catastrophic to you."

"If it were just feelings and not real life then it wouldn't be so scary."

"You had a dream about a little boy in danger, then you had a dream about a woman in black and an earthquake, and this time it was about danger, a coffin and fire. Do you see a pattern?"

"Zoe, please! Can you warn her or something? Are you going to tell her about me?"

I know she's in danger and I've already helped her. "As I've told you before, I would never talk to one of my clients about another client. That would be a serious breach of confidentiality."

"But what if something is so confidential that I'm the only one who knows about it? Because of my powers, you know? Could you at least warn her? Could you tell her what I said?"

She is testing boundaries and it must be some kind of a weird coincidence that she came up with the candles. She mentioned Satan. Perhaps this is some kind of religious delusion. "No, Diana, I can't tell her what you said. We need to spend your time in here talking about you."

"This is about me! That's why I'm here. These visions are making me crazy!"

"Diana, I want you to think about what you're saying. When you first came to see me you did not come here to talk about people in the waiting room. You came here because of your own problems and that's what we need to focus on in here: you and your feelings. That's the nuts and bolts of your therapy."

Diana broke into tears. "All you ever talk about is feelings! Every other word you say is feelings! You want to talk about my feelings? OK, fine! I'm feeling like no one understands. I'm feeling disappointed because you don't understand either. Not really. I'm feeling lost in the forest in the middle of a thunderstorm, trying to find a tree to hide under, but I don't know where the lightning will strike next. I don't know what I can do or where I can go for help if you can't help me. All you keep doing is asking me how I feel and repeating what I say like a parrot. It doesn't matter what I feel! The catastrophes are all going to happen anyway. No one is taking me seriously. This is even worse than my dreams. This is a living nightmare."

"I hear you loud and clear. You're feeling powerless and angry," Zoe soothed.

Diana heaved a long, shaky sigh. "Powerless, angry and desperate. But I can't give up! I have to make you understand. You want to understand, don't you?"

"Yes, I do. And I hear that you're working hard, struggling to be heard. We'll keep working on this together. Can you hang in there with me here while we work together on that?" Zoe asked gently. *Can you hang in there with me until I can figure out what in the hell is going on here?*

"I don't have anywhere else to go. At least you care. You don't always get it, but at least I can tell that you care." Diana looked up at Zoe, her eyes full of entreaty. "Just warn her. You don't have to believe me, but she does. Just warn her that she is in danger. That's all I ask. Help her."

I've already tried, Diana. "Stormy skies subside and the sun always returns eventually. We can ride out this storm together. OK?"

"OK. Just put up the storm warning flags. I don't want anyone else to get hurt."

CHAPTER 21

Rebecca Wentworth and Stephen Jenkins

"*H*e's coming to the front door!" Leah announced as she looked out the large bay window in the family room. "He's so dressed up he looks older! Why is he coming to the front door? He always comes in through the garage."

"Yeah, but this is different. I didn't want him to walk by all the smelly garbage cans so I locked the outside door so he couldn't come in through the garage. You answer it, OK, Leah?" Rebecca said.

"Don't take off right away, 'Becca. I want to take some pictures," Zoe said, grabbing her camera.

"Mom, no, please!" Rebecca said in alarm.

"Come on now. Jessica made me promise I would get some pictures of the two of you together. It isn't every day that you go to a formal."

"Mom, no! Don't even talk to him! Please?"

Stephen rang the doorbell and Leah raced to open the door. "You have to come in because Mom wants to take your picture," Leah said, as Rebecca cringed from the other room.

Stephen came in and said, "Sure," as he awkwardly handed the corsage box to Rebecca who had just peeked around the corner.

Rebecca opened it and saw delicate pink rose buds surrounded by a few leaves of greenery, some baby's breath, and a pink satin ribbon.

"Here. Let me put it on for you," Stephen said, grabbing back the box, trembling and fumbling with pins for what seemed like an eternity, as he unsuccessfully attempted to fasten it to Rebecca's dress. Zoe rescued him by offering to do it for him and he seemed only too eager to have some help. Zoe had told Jessica at work what Rebecca was wearing to the dance so she could tell Stephen what to get for the corsage.

Rebecca's gown was beautiful. It was a sweet, pale pink organza with a fitted pink satin bodice. Two organza rosebuds graced each shoulder and the back was finished with a large satin bow. Her shoes were pale pink satin slippers decorated with a small pink satin bow, tiny roses and little clusters of pearls. Zoe had taken Rebecca to a wedding shop to get an outfit for the dance. Rebecca had announced, "I am not wearing pink!" before they even arrived at the shop, adding, "and I don't want some big puffy thing that looks like a ruffled lamp shade, either. I want something cool and sophisticated." Zoe spotted the dress first and was surprised when Rebecca chose it and tried it on. "What do you think, Mom?" Rebecca had asked. "I really didn't want to wear pink, but this dress is really pretty and I think Stephen would like it."

"Well, 'Becca, it's very lovely, but of course it's completely up to you," Zoe said cautiously, not wanting to tip her hand.

"I'm not sure. It looks kind of babyish, like a little girl's party dress," Rebecca said.

"It almost looks more white than pink, 'Becca, because it's such a pale shade of pink and it's perfect for someone your age. There are plenty of years left for you to wear sexy, sophisticated gowns, but you'll only be sweet sixteen once, so why not take advantage of it?"

"Jeesh, Mom. You're so cheesy!" Rebecca laughed, but she eyed the dress in the mirror and decided to purchase it after the twenty-something sales clerk told her that it showed off her slender waist, that it wasn't babyish at all, and that she thought it was the prettiest dress in the shop.

Rebecca's long hair was French braided with pink satin ribbons at the beauty parlor and once they got home Zoe spent over an hour and a half hand sewing tiny pink satin roses onto the sections of ribbon that were exposed between each plait of hair. Rebecca admired the results by holding a small hand-held mirror in front of her aimed at the large bathroom mirror behind her. "Wow, Mom. You were right. It is cheesy but it's really pretty too. Thanks!"

"You really look awesome!" Leah chimed in. "You look just like Cinderella when she went to meet Prince Charming at the castle."

"And I guess that makes you one of the evil step-sisters," Rebecca said, but she was secretly pleased by her sister's approval.

Daniel came downstairs summoned by the doorbell chime. Despite Rebecca rolling her eyes at Stephen as Zoe posed them for pictures, Rebecca enjoyed every bit of the attention. Daniel quietly took some videotape of the young pair, stopping only to surreptitiously wipe a tiny tear from the corner of his eye so that he could see more clearly through the viewfinder.

"Don't feel bad," Stephen reassured Rebecca once they were finally on their way and out of earshot. "My mom and Anna must have taken a thousand pictures before I even left the house."

"My mom took out old photo albums and showed Leah and my dad pictures of the two of us playing outside together when we were two or three. I think my mom graduated from cheese school or something."

"My mom even made me hold the baby while she took a picture of us and then Anna said, 'Don't shake her, Stevie. We wouldn't want her to throw up all over your tuxedo!'" Stephen imitated Anna's high-pitched voice and Rebecca giggled in appreciation.

"They've probably been plotting this since we were in diapers ourselves!"

"'Rents! They're all the same. They love embarrassing us. What are you going to do?"

"Have fun!" Rebecca said.

CHAPTER 22

Diana's Nightmare

iana was shaking like a Chinese lantern in the middle of an earthquake. She had been up for hours, awakened by chilling images that jolted her from sleep. She was staring at the clock, which changed so slowly that time itself seemed suspended. Her sheets were twisted, wrinkled snakes that slithered across the bed and spilled onto the floor. Every time she fell back to sleep, she returned to unfamiliar territory inside her own mind. Her mouth tasted like pond decay, and her dry, swollen tongue found a hole she had ground through her mouth guard. She yanked it out of her mouth, reached for the phone on her night stand, and knocked the alarm clock onto the floor. She punched in numbers ferociously, as if she were stabbing the images from her dream. *Roz, please be home. Please answer.*

"Hello?" Roz croaked.

"Rozzie! Are you awake?"

"Jesus, Diana. What in the hell time is it?"

"Five eighteen," Diana said, twisting her neck to read the time off of the floor.

"Christ Almighty! What's the matter?" Rozzie said, alarm rising in her voice like a thousand bubbles popping on the surface of a Diet Coke.

"I had another bad dream." Her voice was high pitched with terror.

"Oh, no! What is it this time?"

"You know the crazy guy I told you about with all of the candles?"

"How could I forget?"

"Well, he wants to kill his wife and take the little boy. They tried to escape. They left him, and when he came home and found out they were gone he went into this horrible rage."

"Well, doesn't this mean that the woman and the little boy are safe?"

"I don't know. That's just the thing. I really don't know. I only get bits and pieces. Roz, these psychic dreams are really scaring me, especially since I saw the woman in Zoe's office. They're real. I just know they're real but nobody will believe me. They're so weird and creepy! I just can't take it anymore." Diana started crying into the phone.

"Maybe you should call Zoe. You sound pretty upset."

Diana was gasping for air between sobs. "Zoe doesn't believe me. She thinks it's all about me. She tells me that every character in the dream is part of myself. And I understand that when it comes to regular dreams. But in the dreams where I see these other people, I just know things that I shouldn't know. Things I don't want to know. He's going to find her and kill her. I have to warn her!"

"If she sees Zoe could you tell Zoe to warn her?"

"Zoe said she won't talk to one client about another client. Something about confidentiality. The woman is already gone, anyway. It's too late."

"Well, maybe he won't find her, if she's already gone," Roz said.

"I hope you're right. I thought of calling the police. After all, I know what she looks like and I know what he looks like. I could give a description. But what am I going to say, 'I had a bad dream and you have to do something about it? I'm calling to report a crime that hasn't even happened yet?' They will just think I'm crazy. And maybe

I am crazy. I just don't know anymore." Diana was weeping into the phone.

"Rozzie?

"Ummm?"

"You sound like you're still asleep."

"Asleep? Why would I be asleep at five o'clock in the morning?"

"I'm sorry I woke you. I just didn't know what else to do."

"Don't worry about it. I told you that you can call me at any time, night or day if you were having a rough time. I told you that and I meant it."

"Thank you. You're such a good friend." Diana said, ripping Kleenex out of the box and blowing her nose.

"You know you'd do the same for me if I needed you."

Diana could hear Roz snoring lightly. "Rozzie, I still haven't told you the worst part. Rozzie? Wake up!"

The snoring stopped. "I'm awake. I'm listening."

"Remember how I told you it was like I was the little boy in the last dream?"

"Yeah."

"Well, this time I was this crazy man. I was inside his head and I felt his coldness and loneliness. It's like I actually felt what it's like to be him. He is completely empty inside, devoid of any love or feeling, like everything that is good and pure just doesn't exist for him. He wants to kill this woman because if he can't own her and incorporate her life into himself then he feels empty inside. He's like a black hole in space trying to suck everyone and everything into him so that he owns their power in order to boost up his own. He thinks the only way he can keep her is to kill her. Is that sick or what?"

"How do you know what he's thinking? Do you feel like you're really inside the head of this lunatic?"

"No. It's more like I project myself into him and feel what he is feeling from the inside out."

"But you know that you're not him, right?" Roz asked gingerly.

"Of course. For God's sake, Roz! I'm not insane!"

"I know that, Diana. But you should think about what this sounds like. I'm really worried about you. I think you should call Zoe."

"I feel so sorry for him. He is in so much pain and anguish that he wants to release his rage to get rid of it. It's not going to work, but I understand what he is trying to do. It's even more terrifying than the dream where I was the little boy. I felt trapped inside his cold evil and it stuck to me, like I was defiled and contaminated by it."

"That's awful."

"It was. But the weirdest thing was feeling sorry for him."

"Well, don't feel too sorry for him."

"I never thought about the emptiness inside a criminal before. But I also feel so sorry for the poor little boy and his mother. What's going to happen if she comes home? Somebody has to warn her."

"Diana, listen to me. How long have you been awake thinking about all of this?"

"A few hours, off and on."

"O.K. You're making this mean something. What are you making this mean?"

"Roz, please spare me the psychobabble from that personal growth seminar you took, will you? I need you to be my friend right now. Please stop spouting that 'what are you making this mean?' crap, will you? Ever since you went to that Goddamned seminar I feel like I'm not even talking to you, anymore. I feel like I'm talking to that stupid 'What are you making this mean?' cult. It's like you've been abducted by aliens or something!"

"I told you before, Diana, it's not a cult and there's no need to worry about me. You're making it mean that it's a cult by the story you're telling yourself. But listen, I'm really worried about you. O.K. Let's see. What time is it? I think if I get ready fast we can meet for coffee before work. Let's meet at Dunkin' Donuts and talk about this face to face."

"Which Dunkin' Donuts? The one in Marlborough or the one in Westborough?"

"The one in Westborough is closer to work and that way I don't have to backtrack."

"O.K. The one on the eastbound side of Route Nine or the one across the street from it on the westbound side?"

"I don't care. Whichever one you want."

"I can't think straight."

"Let's go to the one on the westbound side. The side headed towards Worcester. Not the one headed towards Boston. O.K.?'

"My God, it's like Dunkin' Donuts is taking over the world. They have one on every corner. It's hard to decide."

"This really isn't a hard decision, Diana! We're meeting at the one in Westborough on the westbound side of Route Nine, O.K.?"

"What time?"

"As soon as you can get there."

"As soon as you can get there or as soon as I can get there? It's going to take me longer."

"Diana, listen to me. Get dressed and ready for work. Drive to the Dunkin' Donuts as soon as you can get there, and I'll be there by the time you arrive." Roz sounded exasperated.

"Hey Rozzie. One more thing."

"What?"

"Don't make it mean anything."

CHAPTER 23

Joe Ormond

$\mathcal{J}$oe was in a foul mood. He was fantasizing about revenge as he arrived home, slamming the door as he got out of his truck. He had been arguing with Jerry, his boss, about getting a raise. Jerry told him that he was going to have to change his attitude before he would get his raise. *That butt-fuck is not going to screw me out of what he owes me.* Joe imagined himself punching Jerry's face until the image was pulverized. He shoved the key into the lock and kicked open the front door. Joe was surprised that little Joey did not run up to greet him when he opened the door. "Tina, where is Joey?" he called out without receiving a response. He sniffed the air like an animal hunting for prey. He didn't smell food cooking. He quickly went into the kitchen and saw that there was no sign of his dinner being prepared. *Something is up. I have that bitch trained better than this!* He grabbed and loosened his belt buckle in preparation, expecting to find Tina promptly in order to deliver another beating. She knew how he felt about his dinner being ready for him when he got home from work.

Blood pumped into his face and his penis throbbed and grew as he began to fantasize about whipping Tina's smooth white ass until stripes of blood decorated it. "Tina!" he bellowed, looking to see if she were in the bathroom, the bedroom, or Joey's room. It didn't take long for him to come to an amazing conclusion. Not only was his dinner not ready for him, but Tina and Joey were not even home.

Joe's jaw muscles tensed and bulged rhythmically as he clenched his teeth. He began to breathe like a snorting bull. He looked everywhere for a note explaining their absence but he found nothing. "Tina! You fucking bitch!" he bellowed to the walls. His fists were tightening, his heart was pounding, and he felt like he had to hit something. He punched a hole in the wall then roared in pain as he looked at his bloody knuckles. *Now look at what that cunt has done to me!* A rolling boil of rage and panic struck him as he heard his own thunderous heartbeat pounding in his ears. *She better not have left me after everything I've given her.* He looked at the homemade coffin that sat on the floor in the middle of the living room and remembered his mother's coffin being lowered into the ground. He became even more enraged as he felt stabbing grief that she, too, was gone. *How could Mom have done this to me? How could she just kill herself and leave me?* He quickly pushed away thoughts of Mom that created an intolerable level of vulnerability and loss.

I want my son! Where has that bitch taken my son! Joe paced frantically up and down the hall and then went into the kitchen and got himself a six-pack of beer. He tried to think of someone he could call to find out where Tina and Joey had gone, but his mind was so full of the rising steam of anger that he felt like his head was going to explode. *Where are my wife and kid? What if Joey is hurt? What if he's at the hospital?* He flicked on the news but heard nothing about any local accidents. *I'm alone. No one is here to make my dinner.*

His hands were shaking as he grabbed the matches and began lighting candles surrounding the homemade coffin and the altar he had made to the Blessed Mother and to his own mother. He looked long and hard at her smiling picture. *How could you do this to me, Mom?* He saw flashbacks of Mom in her coffin at the wake, her waxy face revealing that she had left him for good. *That's the story of your life. Your body was there, Mom, but you weren't.* Joe remembered

Mom coming home drunk in the middle of the night, staggering into her bedroom with some other drunk while Joe had to fend for himself. That funeral was so unbearable, with everyone whispering about why she had committed suicide. He began weeping but stopped himself. *That fucking whore Tina is not going to turn me into a crybaby.*

He sat watching the news and finished the six-pack. There was still no word from Tina. He called all of the local hospitals and no one had admitted Tina or Joey. He got back in his car and drove around French Hill, looking up and down all the streets of the neighborhood. *The only place she ever goes is the library and the grocery store.* He went to the library but it was closed. Then he drove all around Marlborough, searching up and down Route 20. He went to Price Chopper and called out for Tina and Joey up and down the aisles. He went up to the customer service desk and asked the clerk, "Have you seen a small dark-haired woman with a little boy about three?"

"I've probably seen a hundred women with little boys today. Do you want me to page them?" The pimple-faced clerk revealed a pierced tongue as he spoke.

"Yeah, sure. Page them. Tina and Joey. Go ahead."

"Would Tina and Joey please come to the customer service desk? Your party is waiting for you. Tina and Joey to the courtesy desk, please."

They waited for several minutes but got no response. Joe looked up and down every aisle again. There was no sign of them.

Joe thought of driving to the police station to file a missing person's report until he realized he was probably over the legal limit for blood alcohol. *I'd better keep the fucking cops out of this. She'll probably be there when I get home, anyway.*

Joe got back into the car, grabbed a tape, punched on the tape deck and shoved it in. "London Bridge is falling down, my fair lady. Take the keys and lock her up. Lock her up. Lock her up. Take the keys and lock her up. My fair lady." *What the fuck? How many times have I told that bitch to keep Joey's tapes separate from mine? Oh, this ass whipping is going to be good. I can hardly wait to give her what she deserves after what she's done to me.* He arrived back at the apartment and screeched into the parking space. He rubbed his bloody knuckles as he took them off the steering wheel and winced as he took his folding hunting knife out of his pocket. He stopped at the tree beside the back door entrance to the building and cut off a thick switch, ripping and slicing off the leaves and branches. He carefully smoothed out the switch and smiled in satisfaction as he heard the whistling wind as he whipped the air. *I'm giving her a choice tonight. The belt first and then the switch, or the switch first, and then the belt. Maybe afterwards I should heat things up with a little fire applied to her wounds to cauterize them before I punch her fucking lights out!*

The apartment was still silent and the small, chipped statue of the Virgin Mary looked down on the coffin, which was barely lit by the candles that were just dying out. Before Joe could turn on the light he saw the blinking red light on the answering machine. *Tina must have called to explain where in the hell she is. This had Goddamned well better be good.*

"Hello, Tina? It's Maria. If you're home, pick up." Joe's mind raced wildly as Maria's voice paused. "I hope Zoe could help you. When you get this message, call me."

CHAPTER 24

Zoe, Rebecca and the Butterfly

Zoe was in the kitchen seasoning a roast and putting sweet pota-toes in the oven, preparing a simple meal that would cook itself.

"Mom, I'm going to tell you something and you're not going to like it," Rebecca said, earnestly looking Zoe straight in the face. Zoe began an internal Internet search of every possible subject she knew that Rebecca might categorize in this way. Her anxiety mounted, fueled by both her personal and professional knowledge of the kind of trouble teenagers could get into.

"What?"

"Promise me you won't get mad."

"Rebecca, how in the world can I promise you that I won't get mad when I don't even know what you're going to tell me?"

"Well, just remember, it's my body and I can do what I want with it." Rebecca said, crossing her arms in front of her and tossing her long brown hair with a flick of her head. Zoe began shaking the water out of the salad greens, got out the French knife and the acrylic cutting board and began chopping carrots with vigor.

"O.K., I'll remember that, and I hope you'll remember that your body started out in my body, so I might have some feelings about anything that might endanger or harm it."

"Mother! This is what I mean when I say you don't even trust me! Why are you talking as if I am a newborn baby or something? It's really no big deal, anyway!"

"And what exactly is this 'no big deal' that I'm 'not going to like'?"

"I got a tattoo," Rebecca said, looking away to avoid eye contact with her mother.

"What?" Zoe managed through the jumble of relief and outrage she was feeling. *She's not pregnant, she's not on drugs, she's not prostituting herself, she hasn't attempted suicide and she hasn't gotten arrested. Thank God for small favors. How dare she get a tattoo!*

Rebecca darted quick glances at her mother to check her response in order to gauge how much trouble she was in.

"Rebecca, you know Dad and I don't approve of you mutilating and defacing your body. Not only is it against Jewish law, but your father and I have been very clear about our expectations of you about this. You asked us, we said no, and now you have just gone ahead and disobeyed us. I am very disappointed and angry."

"See! I knew you'd get mad! I didn't even have to tell you, you know!" Rebecca furrowed her brow and puffed out her lower lip.

"You're right. You didn't have to tell me. But that would have changed our relationship. We have always been honest with each other."

"Mom, I know how you and Dad feel about tattoos, and I knew you'd be angry if I went ahead and did it. But then I realized it's my body and I'm not willing to have you and Dad control me like that. I'm not a child anymore. You want to see it? It came out so cool! It's a butterfly."

Zoe loved butterflies and Rebecca knew it. Rebecca pulled down the edge of her soft cotton blouse gently. "See? It's only a small, pretty butterfly and it's on my shoulder so I can easily cover it up with clothes if I ever want to." Zoe had to admit that it was beautifully done, with multiple subtle colors, and she tried to compare it to all of the other possible things Rebecca might have done to herself so that she would be able to accept it.

"Rebecca, what are Bubbe and Zayde going to say about this?"

"Probably the same thing you did."

"You know, when I was a teenager back in the sixties I remember wondering what our kids would do to rebel in the future. I couldn't imagine anything more far out than what we did back then. Who could have imagined something like this? In my day, only drunks and sailors got tattoos."

"Mom, times are changing. Tattoos aren't just for sailors anymore, and not just for guys, either. You say it all the time, Mom. Don't you say that you believe that girls should be able to do what guys do? Aren't you always telling me I should do what I want and not let stereotypes about what girls should or shouldn't do hold me back?" Rebecca looked into her mother's eyes, her pupils slowly widening.

"When we were fighting for the rights of women, I'm not sure we thought that our daughters would become so liberated that they would grow up to get tattoos. It's so primitive. It's so permanent. It's so uncouth!"

"Uncouth! That's a good one! Mom, are you hearing yourself? That's such an old-fashioned word!" Rebecca said.

"Well, it is uncouth! Where did you get this done? How do you know it was safe? What if you were exposed to HIV or Hepatitis C?"

"Mom, I watched the guy take the needle out of the package it came in myself. He used brand new latex gloves. He knew what he was doing. I've known about HIV since elementary school: give me a little credit! What did you expect, that I had some drug addict do it in a back alley?"

"Honestly, I don't know what to expect, Rebecca! I didn't expect this of you, I can say that for sure! Permanently desecrating and marring your body! I hate thinking about it."

"Mom, you tell me that I need to be responsible for the decisions I make about my body, and that I should always stop and consider the consequences of my actions. You say that I shouldn't allow myself to be pressured into things by my peers. I did make a responsible decision, and I just wish you could see that."

"Did your friends pressure you into this?"

"No, Mom. It was my idea. In fact, originally, I was going with Sabrina and Jen to give them moral support. I had no intention of getting a tattoo because I knew you and Dad didn't want me to. But then Jen chickened out."

"Jen was the one who brought you there and then she chickened out? So how many kids got tattoos?"

"That was the funny thing. Just me. And before we got there I was the one saying that I wasn't going to get one. But when I saw all the beautiful designs in the shop, I realized it would be totally cool."

"Where did you go?"

"We went to Rhode Island. Jen's boyfriend knew a really awesome artist there. I told you we were going down to Providence to go shopping, remember? I just didn't say where."

"Don't you have to be an adult to get a tattoo without your parents' permission?"

"Well, yeah, but I look like an adult when I put on make-up. You know how people are always thinking I'm older when I wear make-up."

"I am really having a hard time with this Rebecca! I look at it. I see it's pretty. But I am not happy that you disobeyed me and I am not happy that my daughter has a tattoo." Zoe looked at her own reflection in the black microwave oven door, and she saw that she was puffing out her lower lip and furrowing her brow in an expression that was remarkably similar to the one she had just seen on Rebecca's face.

"Mom, you even admitted it's pretty. The guy told me to put antiseptic ointment on it. It was all very hygienic. He told me how to take care of it, and everything. You would have been pleased if you had been there."

"You wouldn't have gotten it if I had been there," Zoe said, tapping her foot.

"Well, you know Mom, it's too late now. It's like you're always telling me, when you can't change reality you need to adjust to it."

"You were counting on that, weren't you?"

"What do you mean?"

"I mean that I know you and I know that you realized that there would be nothing I could do about it once it was already done, and that's why you did it behind my back. It feels sneaky and manipulative to me."

"Mom, I wouldn't have had to sneak if you just tried to understand. It's what all the kids want. Remember when you told me how you used to iron your hair because it was a fad to have totally straight hair in the hippie days and how Bubbe got mad at you and told you that you were going to burn yourself? It's the same thing, isn't it? Can't you remember how important it is to keep in style? I really did give it a lot of thought and we just have a difference of opinion. But it's my body, and I decided to disobey you because I did not believe that you had the right to stop me from doing something that is safe that makes me feel pretty. C'mon, Mom. All my friends think you're cool. So please, be cool! O.K?"

"I'm glad to hear your friends like me, but I am doing an important job as your parent, and I don't intend to do it any differently in order to win a popularity contest. What is Dad going to say about this?"

"I already talked to him. I called him at work."

"What did he say?"

"He said that he didn't like it, but that you were going to *plotz* when you heard this!"

"Well, he got that one right."

"Believe me, Mom. He was a piece of cake compared to you. Are you going to punish me for disobeying you?"

"Yes, of course I'm going to punish you. You deliberately disobeyed your father and me and you did something impulsively which permanently mars your body. You are grounded."

"But, Mom…"

"You're grounded for two weeks with no phone, TV or music privileges."

"Mom! A week is enough! Two weeks is torture. I have to listen to music, at least, or I won't be able to stand being alone like that."

"I think you'll survive."

Leah burst through the kitchen door, returning from her friend's house. "Thanks for the ride, Mrs. Roberts," she called out, and then she stopped and gasped at the sight of the tattoo on her sister's shoulder.

"A butterfly! That's so cool! Mom, can I get one too?"

"No!" Rebecca and Zoe both said in unison, finally in agreement.

CHAPTER 25

Tina, Joey and Superman

Tina and Joey settled into a comfortable but shabby room at the shelter in Providence only four days after they had first arrived at the safe house. There had been so many changes of location in such a few days that Tina felt lost and disoriented. One moment she was relieved and grateful to think that she didn't have to feel afraid anymore. She was finally freed, unfettered from the heavy anchor of suppressed terror that held her submerged and unable to breathe. The next moment she felt alone and small, adrift in a tiny lifeboat, bobbing on the waves of a vast and endless sea, unsure of how to get to shore.

The abrupt changes left her feeling bewildered and hurt that her marriage had come to this. However pathetic her marriage had been, at least she was part of an intact family. She cried for hours, alone in her room with her face buried in the pillow after Joey was asleep. She missed Joe like she had missed the bus, waiting at the bus stop with no sense of how she could get where she was going. And where was that? Joe had been gone for so long, transformed into a frightening stranger, that Tina could barely remember the remnants of him, let alone imagine the destination of her own shattered life. She felt an aching longing for her dead parents and the familiarity of her childhood home. Joey would have to grow up without his father, and despite everything, Joe had always been good to Joey. She prayed for guidance but felt like her soul was stained with sin, tainted by the rupture of her son's family.

The other women in the morning meeting were able to talk about their situations during the group sessions, but Tina felt like she still had to hide. Words stayed bound up inside her, unsure if it was safe to come out. Still, as she listened to the others, she felt a gradual decrease in her sense of aloneness. After a week she had found the courage to speak up briefly during group in order to ask where she could attend Mass. She was directed to the Cathedral of St. Peter and St. Paul, a beautiful and historic Catholic Church in Providence. She ventured out to walk to church holding tightly to little Joey, the only connection to Joe that was still a visible part of her life. She instantly liked Father Boudreau, the priest who celebrated Mass, and she lingered in church long enough to be able to talk to him after all of the other parishioners had left the church.

Father Boudreau knelt down until he was eye level with Joey who was fingering the wooden railing of the church pew, sticking his little fingers into the curves of the decorative carving.

"How are you doing, little buddy?"

"Good."

"And what have you been up to?"

"I been up to the sky! I'm Superman!" Joey said.

"They have a videotape of the Superman movie at the shelter. Ever since he saw it, he wants to be Superman. He wants to watch it every day," Tina explained.

"You must be very strong if you're Superman," the priest said. Joey was swaying as he rocked back and forth, turning onto the side of his right shoe.

"You know what?" Joey said.

"What?"

"I got a secret!"

"People tell me their secrets all the time. Would you like to tell me yours?" Father Boudreau said, smiling.

"Daddy hurt Mama with big boo-boos. Mama was crying. We didn't saided bye-bye to Dada, we just runded away. He was scary and he screamded at us. Now I gotted more braver 'cause I'm Superman. I can fly away! Daddy can't be a bad boy and hurt us any more. Can we go home now, Mama? I miss Dada."

"We are home, Joey," Tina said.

"Oh, Mama, you're silly! We don't live in the church."

"No, we don't honey, but we live at the shelter now."

"Can Daddy come live with us at the shelter?"

"No, sweetheart. Daddy has to live near his work."

"If I was a bad boy would you run away from me too, Mama?"

"No, sweetheart. Of course not! You will live with Mama until you grow up," Tina said, taken aback by Joey's question.

"Even if I was a bad boy like Daddy?" Joey said, his big brown eyes beseeching his mother.

"Even if you were a bad boy, Mama would never run away from you. Mama is always going to be here to take care of you. But you keep trying to be good, O.K.?"

"I am good, Mama! I'm Superman! Is Superman a good boy?"

"Yes, Joey, Superman is a very good boy."

"Mama, who is the man on the stick?"

"That's Jesus, Our Lord. The stick is called a crucifix."

"Is Jesus a good boy, Mama?"

"Yes, honey. Jesus is a very good boy. Will you try to be good like Jesus?"

"No, Mama! I'm good like Superman!" Joey said, eyeing the crucifix suspiciously.

Tina turned once again to the priest. "He's so innocent. It breaks my heart to see what this has done to him. Joe really loves him and Joey knows it. He misses his father." Tina began to weep, covering her face with her hands. "Father, when I think of how hard this is on

Joey, I wonder if I'm in a state of mortal sin for leaving my husband. I don't even know if I should receive Communion. I know Our Lord did not approve of divorce. I just didn't know what else to do. I had to protect my son."

"Our Lord would have wanted you to do exactly as you have done," Father Boudreau said. "You have sought refuge and sanctuary for your child and yourself in order to protect life. The Church puts the sanctity of life even above the sacrament of marriage. In our courtyard, in front of this church, set in stone, you will see a passage from the Bible, found in the Old Testament, in Deuteronomy. 'I have set before you life and death, the blessing and the curse. Choose Life then, that you and your descendants may live.' Next to this is the image of Our Lady caressing her young Son, trying to protect Him, as you have tried to protect your little boy. God knows that you did not make this decision lightly. You gave thoughtful consideration to the vows of your marriage and you prayed for guidance. You had a most difficult dilemma, and you made the best choice you could. In a situation like this, leaving your husband is not a sin, and I see no reason that you should not receive Communion. Your husband's violence left you no other choice. Perhaps we could pray for Joe."

"Yes. I'd like that," Tina said sadly.

"Joey, would you like to say a prayer for your father?" Father Boudreau said, moving closer to the child. Joey didn't answer but grabbed the back of his mother's jeans and hid behind her. Father Boudreau patted Joey's head. "Heavenly Father, we ask that You protect this woman and child and keep them safe from harm. We also ask that You move the heart of Joey's father, Joe, to release him from the evil that has taken his heart hostage. May he turn away from the darkness and seek the Light of Your holy love." Tina and the priest crossed themselves as Joey took a tiny plastic dinosaur out of his pocket and moved it along the top of the old oak pew. "In the name of the Father, and of the Son and of the Holy Spirit. Amen." A sacred hush set upon the three briefly, until Joey roared for his Tyrannosaurus Rex.

"Thank you, Father," Tina said, smiling at her son as she held on to the top of the oak pew, worn smooth by the all of the hands that came before hers.

"That's what I'm here for," Father Boudreau said. "God bless you, and feel free to come by whenever you like."

"Good thing I'm not afraid of those fires," Joey said loudly as he slowly inched his way closer to the votive candles. "I'm Superman, and I'm not afraid of anything!" Joey put his arms in front of him and he flew down the long aisle, into the sunshine that awaited them outside.

CHAPTER 26

Zoe and Diana

*D*iana hung back a little as Zoe opened the door to her office. Diana heaved a long, weary sigh before she arranged herself on the couch.

"She's gone, isn't she?" Diana asked as she looked squarely into Zoe's clear blue eyes.

"Gone?" Zoe asked quietly.

"That woman. The one I told you is in danger. You don't see her anymore, do you?"

"As I've mentioned before, it would be unethical for me to talk to you about anyone else's treatment, or even to acknowledge whether or not someone else is a client."

"I understand. That's okay. I know it, anyway. He's still very dangerous but she's gone, so it doesn't matter. I have to look on the bright side. No matter what he wants to do to her he can't do it if she's gone. I need to remember that."

"Are things feeling safer to you now?" Zoe asked gently.

"Not really. It's going to get a lot worse before it gets better. I don't know if it can be avoided. I mean, I can at least somewhat influence what goes on in my head when I'm awake. But these dreams usually happen when I'm asleep so there's really no way I can control what happens in my dreams."

"Hmmm."

"And then when things happen in real life, I feel like it's my fault somehow. The other day I was so scared that I called Roz in the middle of the night. She is such a good friend. Can you believe that she actually met me at Dunkin' Donuts at the crack of dawn just because I had another nightmare? Like they always say, 'A friend in need is a friend indeed.' Anyway, there I was, crying into my hazelnut coffee, right in the middle of Dunky's. I'm always crying in restaurants these days. But before long Roz had me laughing again. That's what I love about Roz."

"She sounds like a very supportive friend."

"She is. She's always making me laugh and put things in perspective. She's the one who also pointed out to me that if this lunatic is looking for that other client and if he's in a rage that he can't find her so he can kill her, then that probably means that she got away okay. I even think the little boy is safe too. So do you think I can stop worrying about her?"

"I feel confident that it will begin to feel safe enough for you to let go of your fear around that."

"She got away and she's okay?"

"Hmmm."

"I don't feel so confident."

"I know. Please feel free to borrow some of my confidence while you're working on building your own," Zoe offered.

Diana shifted her position on the couch, then looked away from Zoe momentarily before she responded. "O.K. Zoe, I have to tell you the truth here. I come in here and I talk to you and tell you these dreams, but then I keep having them. I don't see how this therapy thing works, anyway. All I do is talk to you the same way I talk to my friends. I was talking to Roz and trying to figure out if there is anything different going on when I talk to her compared to when I talk to you. The only thing I could come up with is the questions. You really are a good question thinker-upper. You ask a different kind of question than my friends ask. But sometimes I worry that I'm not really getting anywhere. I mean, no offense, but nothing has really changed that much about the dreams, so how can I tell? Do you think I'm making any progress?" Diana twirled a strand of her hair.

Zoe sat up straighter in her chair and subtly changed the tone of her voice to indicate the importance of Diana's question. "Well, first of all, it's important to define the problem. The dreams aren't the problem, the dreams are your internal process for resolving the problems. So continuing to have strong and vivid dreams and bringing those dreams into the therapy room so that we can work on them together is a sign that you are working hard, both with your conscious mind and with your unconscious mind. I hope you're able to join me in acknowledging that work. Are you with me so far?" Zoe asked ardently.

"Yeah, I guess so," Diana said doubtfully, as she looked away again.

Zoe paused until Diana was able to return her gaze. "As far as symptoms, we look at three things: frequency, intensity and duration. When we began treatment you described symptoms such as a pounding heartbeat, a feeling that you were floating, panic attacks, difficulty concentrating, and disturbance of sleep, appetite and breathing. The question to ask yourself is whether those symptoms are happening as frequently as they did when you started, whether they are as intense as they were before, how long they last, and how long it takes you to recover from them when they do occur." Zoe sat back in her chair and waited patiently.

"When you put it like that, I guess I have made progress because that feeling that I can't breathe is better, my panic attacks are almost gone and that floaty feeling I told you about doesn't happen very much anymore either. I forgot about that." Diana visibly relaxed, letting her shoulders and neck settle back down.

"You've been working hard in here and that work is paying off for you."

"But I still feel scared to go to sleep at night because I'm afraid of the dreams I'm going to have. That isn't normal, is it?"

"Well, it certainly is understandable that you would feel anxious about falling asleep at night if you know that you're likely to have disturbing dreams. Naturally, that would feel troubling to you."

"And not all of them are so troubling anymore, either. Sometimes they're even funny. Last night I had another dream about the teenage girls. I don't think I ever told you about them, did I?"

"No, I don't believe you did." Zoe looked out the window briefly, watching a squirrel scampering down a tree holding onto an acorn before returning her gaze to Diana.

"Well, I was having one of those recurrent dreams, but this one wasn't even scary at all. In fact, I told Roz about it and we were laughing and saying at least some of these dreams are as silly and ridiculous as they are supposed to be." Diana picked up one of the throw pillows on the couch and held it to herself, hugging it and caressing the fringe around its edges. "Anyway, it was about these two teenaged girls who were singing together in a car. Nothing much ever happens in these dreams, but I have the same two characters in my dreams over and over again." Diana laughed lightly.

"What do you make of that?" Zoe asked, her penetrating blue eyes looking deeply into Diana's.

"I don't know. I never really thought about it much. I mean, these dreams never bothered me the way the other ones did. It just seems like these two teenaged girls hang out together and one is older and one is younger. One is blonde and one is brunette. I don't know if they're friends, or cousins or sisters or what, although in the last one you were in it and you were the girls' mother, so I think they were sisters." Diana picked up the pillow again and felt the texture of its fabric, rubbing her palm over its surface.

"Do you remember how you felt about that in the dream?" Zoe asked, wondering if somehow Diana knew about Rebecca and Leah. *I've never even mentioned that I have children.*

Diana pondered this momentarily, looking up at the ceiling. "I don't think I felt much of anything, really. I think I felt amused in the dream. It always feels sort of nice when I see these two characters also, like isn't that sweet that they hang out and tease each other? I'm telling you, Zoe, I really do have a strange mind. One minute I'm an emotional wreck because of one dream and then another dream happens and I don't even seem to care what happens one way or the other. Oh, and I forgot to tell you the funniest part. They were singing this beautiful song about peace, and God, and right in the middle they stopped and had an argument. It was so silly. They were arguing about which key to sing the song in. Isn't that weird?" Diana tossed the pillow in the air and caught it again before she smiled broadly at Zoe.

Zoe felt the hair on the back of her neck standing up and paying attention. *Oh my God! She's talking about Rebecca and Leah. They were fighting in the car about which key to sing a song in on the way to their Youth Pro Musica rehearsal! Nobody was there except the girls and me. How does she keep doing this? Maybe it's just a coincidence, but how many coincidences can there be? She said I was their mother. I don't care what Jessica or anyone else says. I think she is psychic!*

CHAPTER 27

Joe Ormond and Zoe Wentworth

*J*oe stood for a moment staring at the answering machine, trying to make sense of the message. "Hello, Tina? It's Maria. If you're home, pick up. I hope Zoe could help you. When you get this message call me." He played it over and over again. *Who in the hell is Maria?* Suddenly, it dawned on him. Maria was Rico's mother, the one Tina and Joey knew from story hour at the library. *But who is this bitch Zoe?* He played the message again. *Who helps people? A priest? No, Zoe is a woman's name. A doctor? No, people don't call doctors by their first name. A counselor? Did Tina go to see a counselor?* Joe got the phone book and looked under counselors in the yellow pages. *How can I find out which one it is when I don't even have a last name? Zoe. Zoe. Oh, here it is!* Joe found the name Zoe Wentworth, LICSW, listed along with all the other therapists in a display ad for Hager Pond Counseling Associates. *Hager Pond. That's right here in Marlborough.* Joe called the number listed and he was surprised when someone answered the phone this late in the evening. He asked to speak to Zoe.

"I'm sorry, sir. This is the answering service. Would you like me to take a message or would you prefer to call back in the morning? The office opens at nine."

"I'll call back."

"And your name, sir?"

Joe hung up the phone without answering. *I'd better hit the sack. I'm going to find this Zoe bitch first thing in the morning.* Joe looked at the picture of his mother that he had placed at the head of the coffin. He clenched his jaw, tensing his muscles as he gnashed his teeth. *Fucking women. They all disappear on you one way or the other.* Then he looked away, tossed his grimy green baseball cap across the room and let his blue jeans drop onto the floor before getting into his bed alone.

He slept fitfully, yanking the covers violently and waking with a start every time he realized that he was alone in the bed. He had frustrating dreams that he was trying to beat Tina with a switch but couldn't follow through. He dreamed that he grabbed his belt instead, and his pants fell down. He tried to chase Tina but his pants twisted around his ankles and made him fall. His rage was building as he tried to beat Tina again and again. He longed to see red welts rising on Tina's smooth white skin, but as he frantically tried to beat her she began laughing at him. "You bitch," he screamed. "You fucking cunt! I'll get you!" The more impotent he felt trying to deliver the beating the more angry he became until he woke up with a start. "Tina!" he bellowed, half asleep, but there was no answer.

He threw back the sheets and blankets, got up, and lit a cigarette from the one votive candle that still burned around the coffin. Calmed by the nicotine, he returned to his bed, grabbed his penis and masturbated to the frenzied fantasy of whipping Tina, aroused by imagining the whistling sound of the switch punctuated by her screams. He couldn't fall back to sleep, instead planning revenge and retribution for being so grievously wronged. He got up again, paced back and forth, had another cigarette and looked at the clock, as if willing it to change. He went into Joey's silent room sitting alone with the emptiness. Finally, he fell back to sleep briefly in Joey's room, grasping the pillow on Joey's twin bed, holding it tightly, then wincing at the pain in his knuckles, still covered with dried blood from punching the wall. He began crying, "Joey. Joey. My son!"

By sunrise he lay in bed staring at the dust particles caught suspended mid-air by the morning light, formulating a plan. He called in sick to work, then he waited until eight o'clock to call the counseling center. He asked to speak to the billing department.

"Good morning. I'm wondering if you can help me. My wife, Tina Ormond, goes there for counseling and I have a question about the bill. I'm paying bills and I just wanted to check to make sure that we don't owe you anything."

"One moment. I'll check the computer."

"Thank you. I appreciate it."

"How do you spell the last name?"

"O-R-M-O-N-D, Tina Ormond."

"Oh, here it is. Tina Ormond. She just came in recently. No, you're all set. Your wife paid in cash when she was here. Did you say you got a bill? That must be an error."

"That's okay. We all make mistakes," Joe said, running his tongue over his teeth, as he hung up the phone. He drove straight to the counseling center parking lot and spit into the green scum that covered Hager Pond. Just before nine he walked up to the receptionists' window. "I'm here to see Zoe Wentworth."

"O.K. I'll call her." The receptionist, Lydia Bennet, picked up the phone and called Zoe to come to the waiting room. "Your nine o'clock is here." Lydia had been trained not to say client names out loud in order to insure confidentiality within the waiting room.

"What? I don't even have a nine o'clock today."

"Well, there's a man here to see you and he seems to think he has a nine o'clock appointment with you." Lydia looked up at Joe. "Are you sure it's Zoe Wentworth that you're here to see?"

"Yes."

"And your appointment is for nine o'clock?"

"Yes it is."

"Zoe, he says he has a nine o'clock with you. I don't recognize him. Maybe he's a new client. Did you have a nine o'clock intake scheduled?"

"No, not that I remember. Maybe I do and I forgot to write it down."

"Well, would you come and talk to him?" Lydia slid the frosted glass window closed, lowered her voice and whispered into the phone. "He's giving me the creeps."

"I'll be right there." Zoe came to the front desk and noted Lydia glancing at her with a worried look. Zoe approached the man and offered him a brief business-like nod. "Good morning. I'm Zoe Wentworth. You're here to see me?"

"Uh huh."

"You're a new client here?"

"Well, no actually. I've been thinking about getting some counseling but I'm not sure if I want to or not." Joe's tongue darted out quickly and licked his lips before retreating.

"And why did you ask for me?" Zoe looked perplexed.

"Some guy at work told me that you really helped him a lot. I forget his name."

"Do you have an appointment?"

"No. I just wanted to see you. Can we talk privately?

"No. I'm afraid we don't work that way. If you like, you can schedule an appointment to see me."

"That's good because I really need help."

Zoe turned to Lydia. "Can you help this gentleman get connected with the Intake Department?"

"Sure."

Zoe turned away and returned to her office, leaving Lydia to take care of the rest. Lydia handed Joe a clipboard with paperwork to fill out.

"What's this?" Joe asked.

"Those are the forms we need you to fill out. I thought you might want to take care of that while you're here. You could also do it when you come back after you have an appointment."

"I'd rather do it later."

"O.K. then. Here's a card. Call this number to make an appointment and if you want to see Zoe just tell the Intake Department that when you call."

"Thank you very much. I'll do that."

Joe returned to his truck to wait. He watched cars coming and going all day. Finally, Zoe came out of the building and Joe watched her getting into her car. He followed her, staying far enough behind that she would not know she was being followed. He watched as she pulled up to the Ashcroft School. Two girls got into the car.

Oh good. She has kids. I was hoping she had kids. It's payback time! She took my kid and now she's going to find out what it feels like to lose her kid. Joe followed the car and watched as Zoe and her children got out and went into their house. *This is going even better than I thought. I know where she lives, where her kids go to school and I know where she works. This is going to be a piece of cake. Not bad for a day's work. Not bad at all.*

CHAPTER 28

Thanksgiving at the Wentworths

"Hey, no fair!" Leah said, holding up her hand, displaying black olives adorning each finger. "My hands are getting too big for this. I can barely keep the olives on."

"That should be a clue to you, Leah, that you're getting too old to be sticking olives on your fingers." Rebecca rolled her eyes and looked up at the ceiling contemptuously before shaking her head back and forth slowly.

"That's what olives are for, 'Becca. Otherwise, why would they have these wicked cool little holes in them?" Leah asked.

"That's where they took the pits out, Brainless," Rebecca explained with exasperation.

"What pits? I never saw any pits in olives."

"Oh, my God! You are so clueless! You never saw any pits in olives because Mom always buys the kind where they have already taken the pits out!"

"Really? Is that really why there are holes in the olives, Mom? Are the holes from where they took out the pits?" Leah asked her mother as Zoe walked into the family room with her hands up to her right ear, carefully putting on her turkey earrings.

"Yes, of course, sweetheart. What did you think? Now stop eating them and leave some for the guests."

"Can I just eat the ones that are already on my fingers?" Leah asked.

"Yes, but then that's it," Zoe said firmly.

"Of course you can eat the ones that are already on your fingers! What do you think? Do you think Mom is going to tell you to put them back in the bowl after you've put your grubby little paws all over them?"

"Rebecca, please don't start in with her." Zoe looked at her eldest daughter with warning that left no doubt that Mom meant business.

"What? I'm just trying to teach her some manners!" Rebecca sulked.

"Rebecca, it's not your job to teach her manners. It's my job and it's Dad's job," Zoe said calmly.

"Maybe if you did your job and she actually had any manners I wouldn't have to do your job for you," Rebecca mumbled, almost under her breath, turning to walk away.

"Excuuuuse me! That's enough!" Zoe said angrily. "I will not be spoken to disrespectfully!"

"Sorry. I didn't think you would hear that," Rebecca said contritely, lifting both her eyebrows and crouching slightly.

"Well I did! I think you'd do well to remember that your job is to work on yourself and let others work on themselves."

"O.K., O.K., I said I'm sorry, Mom. Jeesh!"

"She said she's sorry, Mom. Don't rag on her. Anyway, she's right. It really isn't very good manners for me to stick olives all over my fingers and pig out on them before the company comes." Leah said, coming to her sister's aid.

"Thanks, Lee Lee," Rebecca said, using a pet name for her sister that she hadn't used in years.

"Come on, 'Becca. Let's go open the cashews and put them in the leaf dishes," Leah said, steering her older sister away from their mother.

Once safely in the kitchen, Leah said, "'Becca, you have to take a chill pill. Mom is always stressed out when company is coming. Just stay out of her way. That's what I do."

"Good idea, Leah. And thanks for the save."

Just then the doorbell rang. Jessica was holding the diaper bag and a casserole dish covered with dish towels to keep it warm, Anna was holding a bottle of wine and two pink boxes of pies suspended by the string tied around them, and Stephen was carrying Bridget, the baby, in her infant seat.

"Stephen!" Rebecca exclaimed. "I thought you were going to your dad's house for Thanksgiving."

"I was, but I decided I'd rather spend my Thanksgiving with you, so I called and told him." Rebecca's smile was glowing brightly as she whispered, "Thank you" to Stephen.

"It smells wonderful in here!" Jessica exclaimed as Zoe rushed to open the door and helped to carry in some of the dishes.

"It smells like Thanksgiving!" Leah announced.

Daniel came downstairs, tearing himself away from the computer, summoned by all the commotion.

"Dan would you please help Stephen bring in the Port-A-Crib?" Anna asked, putting the pies down on the kitchen table, taking the baby from Stephen and untying her hat.

"Sure. C'mon, Stephen," Dan said, grabbing his coat.

"Girls, could you start gathering some extra chairs around the house?" Zoe asked.

"Sure, Mom," Rebecca said. "C'mon, Leah."

"Let me see. Turkey, stuffing, mashed potatoes, what do you have there, Anna?" Zoe asked.

"Green bean casserole with slivered almonds, sauteed mushrooms and crumbled French fried onions. Can I help with anything?"

"Sounds yummy. Yes, as a matter of fact you can help. Would you put these miniature marshmallows on top of the candied yams so I can run them under the broiler? What am I forgetting? The table is set. The gravy's on the stove. I'll put that in the gravy boat. What else?" Zoe asked.

"The cranberry sauce. I'll get it," Jessica said, peering into the fridge. Do you have it in that turkey dish you always use?"

"Yes. What else? Something's missing. The corn muffins are in the oven staying warm. Butter!" Zoe exclaimed, grabbing the butter dish.

Quickly, everyone pitched in, Rebecca and Leah putting chairs around the table, Stephen setting up the port-a-crib, Dan carving the turkey and arranging it on a serving platter, Zoe putting the food on the table, getting serving spoons, forks and tongs, everyone working in unison, completing final tasks.

"O.K. Let's eat! Come and get it while it's hot!" Dan called out.

"Your parents aren't coming out from California this year?" Anna asked Zoe.

"No. My dad just had hip replacement surgery and they aren't up for the trip. We'll call them later." Zoe surveyed the dining room table for all of the decorative items that belonged on the table: the ceramic turkey, the Indian salt shakers, the corn-shaped candles, and the cornucopia basket decorated with miniature gourds and silk fall leaves, the centerpiece for the table.

"Are we going to go around the table and say what we're thankful for?" Leah asked, putting a Beanie Baby stuffed turkey on the table.

"Sure, honey, that's a family tradition. O.K. everybody. Time to eat!" Dan said. Everyone came to the table and sat down while Anna latched the baby's seat onto the table. "Let's dig in!" Dan said.

"Zoe, I love the way you always bake some jam into the center of the corn muffins. It's so delicious. What kind of jam is it?" Jessica asked.

"Boysenberry. We have to bring in some of our California heritage. Some people out here have never even tasted Boysenberry jam."

"Really? The Pilgrims didn't have Boysenberry jam?" Leah asked.

"Sure, Squanto hopped a plane to Knott's Berry Farm in California and picked up a case on his way to Plymouth," Rebecca said. "That's how the Pilgrims survived that first terrible winter. They ate jam." Zoe looked at Rebecca with warning in her eyes.

"Stephen, I see you're a dark meat man," Dan said.

"Always. The dark meat's the best."

"I prefer the white meat," Jessica said.

"Yeah, Mom and I have been arguing about this for years, but I know the dark meat's the best!"

"I like white meat," Rebecca said. "Especially with Daddy's gravy all over it. Daddy makes the best gravy." Stephen smiled at Rebecca and clasped her hand below the table. Anna and Jessica looked at each other and smiled.

"What kind of pies did you bring?" Leah asked Anna.

"Pumpkin and apple."

"Yummy! Mom, do we have whipped cream to go with it?"

"We sure do. And vanilla ice cream, too," Zoe said, and then gasped, "I just figured out what's missing! I never put out the Jello mold!"

"It wouldn't be Thanksgiving unless we forgot to put something on the table," Dan said. "It's a family tradition."

"You can put it out when we do desserts, Mom," Rebecca said.

"That's a great idea, honey. I'll do that."

"Dessert! You must be kidding. I am more stuffed than the turkey!" Jessica said. "I'll never be able to eat anything again."

"You say that every year, and every year you have dessert," Anna said, picking up a baby spoon that had fallen on the floor.

"Thank goodness we always have dessert later," Jessica said.

"Are we going to play Charades again this year?" Stephen asked.

"Yes! After dinner, let's play Charades!" Leah exclaimed. "Let's do the thankfuls. Can I go first?"

"Sure, honey, go ahead," Zoe said.

"I'm thankful for my family, and I'm thankful that I didn't get Mr. Huffman for math this year, and I'm thankful for all my friends. I'm especially thankful that Mom helped my friend who has an eating disorder, because even though I was mad at you at the time, Mom, she is getting help now, and I'm glad you told on her because now she's stopped barfing all the time."

"Leah, do you have to talk about barfing now?" Rebecca said, wearily. "We're at the table."

"I know, but I'm just doing my thankfuls. What are you thankful for?" Leah retorted.

"I'm thankful that Stephen and I have become closer this year," Rebecca said, blushing. "And I'm thankful for Mom and Dad, and I'm thankful for all my friends, and I'm thankful I have my learner's permit and that I'm going to pass the driving test and get my license very soon!"

Stephen took a second helping of turkey, stuffing and gravy, and whispered to Rebecca, "I'm thankful for you."

"Your turn for thankfuls, Stephen," Leah invited.

"I'm thankful for Mom and Anna, and I'm thankful Rebecca is my girlfriend, and I'm thankful for the baby except when she screams her little head off at four o'clock in the morning. I'm thankful that I made Cross Country this year, and I'm thankful for dark meat, the best meat on the turkey!" Stephen said, smiling broadly as Rebecca looked on, worshipfully.

Bridget began to wail and Jessica saw that she was sinking down in the infant seat. She quickly moved to prop her up.

"Have you got a pillow I could use, Zoe?" Jessica asked.

"Sure, just grab one off the couch in the living room. I'd get one for you but I'm kind of wedged in here," Zoe said.

"Hurry up, she's slipping again," Jessica said, holding her in place until Anna could prop her up again. Once repositioned, the baby settled down.

Leah took another helping of mashed potatoes, created a crater in the middle and poured in some gravy to fill it up. "Your turn for thankfuls, Daddy," Leah said, as Dan poured himself another glass of wine.

"I'm thankful to be here for another year with family and friends. And I'm thankful that we've made it through another year without anything terrible happening," Dan said.

Zoe looked at Dan with surprise. "That's a funny thing to say."

"Not to me. Every year when we gather again, that's always what I'm most thankful for. Life is so unpredictable and terrible things could happen that would change everything. So I'm grateful that we've made it through another year intact."

"Could you pass me another one of those corn muffins, Becca?" Stephen beamed at Rebecca.

"Can I butter it for you, Stephen?" Rebecca asked.

"Oh, brother," Leah said, not quite as far under her breath as she had intended.

Bridget began to fuss again and Anna got her out of her seat, grabbed a bottle from the diaper bag and began to feed her the bottle, stroking her hair.

"Dan, you really outdid yourself. How do you get the white meat to stay so moist?" Jessica asked.

"A little trick I learned from *Joy of Cooking*. I soak cheesecloth in melted butter and then wrap it around the breast meat while it's cooking. It works like a charm."

"Okay, my turn for thankfuls." Zoe said. "I'm thankful for my wonderful husband, who is my favorite chef, and for my two wonderful daughters, and I'm thankful that I am able to help my clients, and for how rich that feels to me. I'm thankful for another year, celebrating Thanksgiving with our friends. And I'm thankful we have a dishwasher!" Zoe said, eyeing all of the dishes.

"Don't worry. I'll help," Jessica said. "I'm thankful for the way you have embraced us as a family, supported us through thick and thin, and welcomed us into your home for Thanksgiving. You are terrific friends and it is an honor to know you. I am thankful for Anna, Stephen, and our new little pumpkin, Bridget. And I'm thankful that love is love and it's a tremendously powerful thing to find, no matter where you find it." Jessica beamed at Anna.

"Thanks, Honey. I'm thankful for you, too. And I'm thankful for our daughter, and our son, and I'm thankful I'm finally out of the closet with my parents, and I'm thankful for how well that went. And I'm thankful for all the love of friends and family. O.K. I guess that's everything."

"And that's everybody," Zoe said.

"No, Mom. What about Bridget?" Leah asked.

Zoe smiled indulgently. "Would you like to do the baby's thankfuls for her, Leah?"

"Sure!" Leah mimicked a high-pitched baby voice and said, "I'm thankful for my bottle, and my pacifier, and I'm thankful that my poopy diapers get changed, and I'm thankful for both of my moms and my big brother. And I'm thankful I'm too little to have to do any chores or homework. And I'm thankful I'm so adorable."

"Thank you, Leah," Jessica said, smiling warmly.

"Can we go play Charades now?" Leah asked.

"Sure, why don't all of you break into teams and start writing down things for the other team to act out? Jessica and I will clear the table and start the first load of dishes. We should be done by the time you're ready to start."

"Okay, Good," Leah said.

"Let's find some paper and pens so we can write things down," Rebecca said. "Who's on which team?" Everyone but Zoe and Jessica left the dining room and went into other rooms to choose teams and to prepare for Charades.

"Jess, I'm glad we're alone. I wanted to ask you something," Zoe said, scraping and rinsing plates and arranging them in the dishwasher. "Have any of your clients ever guessed about your relationships or your kids?"

"No, why?"

"That client I was telling you about had a dream about the girls and me."

"What happened in the dream?"

"Nothing, really. She just described a conversation that Rebecca and Leah had in the car on their way to their rehearsal. She even knew what they were arguing about and she knew that they were singing. How do you explain that?"

"Well, you never know. She could have been in the audience at one of their performances and seen their names in the program. Try to remember how often they sing: in churches, in concert halls, on the radio, and T.V. Just from the names she could have figured out that they were your kids. Did she know their names?

"No, but she knew they were having an argument about which key to sing one of their songs in. And she knew that one was blonde and one was brunette."

"My guess is that this is transferential. After she somehow found out about your daughters at one of their performances she may have some issues about them, like a kind of unconscious sibling rivalry."

"I guess that makes sense. She knows that the girls sing so she just imagines an argument about what key they're singing in. What else do singers argue about? If you think about it, the whole plot of the dream fragment is about sibling rivalry. She even told me that I was their mother."

"If she somehow saw their names and even unconsciously associated them with you, she could be presenting you with a dream in order to find out if you really have kids. She may feel she has to compete with them for your time and attention. Not only that, but keys can be a very powerful dream symbols. Did you explore that with her?"

"No, I think I was too stunned, thinking she really is psychic. But exploring her personal meanings for keys could be very fruitful. That's a good idea. I just couldn't imagine how she could have known about the girls, but you're right, really. Their chorus is performing all over the place. How do I know she wasn't in the audience somewhere? Thanks for your sensible advice, as always. What was that?" Zoe asked in alarm.

"What was what?" Jessica asked quizzically.

"That noise. I heard something." Zoe went to the large bay window in the dining room and peered out into the darkness. "I could have sworn I heard something rustling around in the bushes outside."

"It must have been a dog or something," Jessica said reassuringly. "I don't see anything out there."

Joe crouched down outside the bay window in order to avoid detection. *That was a close call! How nice! The whole family gathered together for Thanksgiving. Enjoy it while you still can.* Joe smiled in satisfaction as he contemplated his next move.

CHAPTER 29

Zoe, Diana and the Butterfly

Diana's terror stricken eyes searched Zoe's and locked in contact, afraid to lose hold of her gaze. Diana's whole body was trembling and her teeth were almost imperceptibly chattering inside her tightly pursed lips. "I, uh, you, um, you…" Diana muttered shakily as she tried to summon speech. Instead, she rubbed her forehead back and forth as if trying to erase what she saw inside her mind. One lone tear streaked down her face and splashed onto her lap as she picked up the throw pillow on Zoe's couch, grasped it in her arms and rocked her body back and forth. "It's all around you, Zoe. I mean it's not you but it feels like it could be you. I'm scared."

"It's me?" Zoe asked.

"In the dream, the nightmare. It's him. The bad guy. It's about to happen. There's danger all around you. I can feel it. We have to stop it."

"I'm perfectly safe and I'm here with you," Zoe said softly, trying to soothe Diana's fears.

"No."

"You're feeling a sense of danger," Zoe said.

"So much has happened but it's going to be worse. You have to believe me!" Diana covered her face with her hands and began convulsing into sobs, gasping for air in loud, ripping inhalations.

"My heart is pounding so loud. Can you hear it? I think I'm having a heart attack!" Diana exclaimed, the pitch of her voice rising almost as high as her eyebrows.

"It sounds like you're in the middle of a panic attack. It feels terrible but you're not having a heart attack, you're having a panic attack. It can't hurt you."

"But I can't breathe!"

Zoe used hushed tones, slowing her voice and modulating her tones using techniques designed to counteract her client's panic. "Slow your breathing. Breathe from the diaphragm. That's right. Slow down. You're doing fine. Calm yourself down. You can make it through. Just ride it out. Ride it out. Slow, deep breaths, you're safe here, you're safe now."

"I don't even know who she is! Oh, my God, my stomach hurts." Diana started crying again and brought her legs up to her chest, crouching in the corner of the sofa.

"Diana, I need you to slow down and start at the beginning. Take slow, deep breaths. You're safe here. Tell me about the nightmare and we'll talk about the scary feelings together. I'm right here with you."

"I think I'm going to be sick."

"Here's the wastebasket. You can use it if you need to and you can't make it to the bathroom in time."

Zoe's matter of fact tone soothed Diana, but she still remained in an almost fetal position, holding on to the wastepaper basket with a tight grip. "It's the teenaged girl from the dream. It's not you but she looks like you. It could be you in the past. I'm not sure. She's sitting in front of her school. There's a big weeping willow tree there. She's there with the same younger kid, maybe her friend or something. He's there, lurking, stalking them. He's been following them for days but they don't know it."

"Who?"

"The bad guy from the other dreams who beats up his wife. The one I was in the other dream. The one who feels cold and empty inside. Remember?"

Joe Ormond! Zoe felt a chill rush through her.

"He wants to kill the teenaged girls and I'm afraid he's going to do it. I can't tell if it's already happened or if it's going to happen. I don't know. I feel like it's happening right now! We have to save her but I don't know where she is or even who she is. But she looks just like you." Diana felt urgent cramping in her abdomen. "I have to go to the bathroom!" Diana said, pushing the door open and running from the office.

Zoe's fear began deep in her bowels and traveled up to tighten her vocal cords, rising like an express elevator, leaving her stomach one floor below. She quickly punched some numbers into the telephone. "Mrs. Randall? This is Zoe Wentworth."

"Yes?"

Please, God. Please be okay. "Are my girls okay there?"

"I believe so. Why, is there a problem?"

"Oh, no. I don't think so. I'm probably just being silly but would you mind just checking on them for me?"

"Certainly." Zoe shook one leg up and down vigorously as she waited for Mrs. Randall to return to the phone. "Mrs. Wentworth? Your girls are right where they ought to be. They're studying in the library as usual. Is something the matter? You don't sound like yourself. Would you like me to give them a message? Are you going to be late?"

"No, I'll be there soon, about the usual time."

"O.K., then."

"Thank you for checking. I appreciate it."

Diana returned to the session looking pale and fragile.

"Are you all right?" Zoe asked, startled by Diana's worsening appearance.

"Yes. I think I'll be okay now. Sorry."

"There's no need to apologize. Do you feel up to continuing?" Zoe asked. *I hope she doesn't. I want to go get the girls and make sure they're safe.*

"Yes! Please, I can't go home," Diana said in alarm. "I'm still too shook up. I have to stay!" Diana's lower lip was quivering.

"You feel shaken." *That makes two of us. Please God! Keep Rebecca and Leah safe.*

"Can I stay?" Diana asked.

"Of course," Zoe said, her heartbeat pounding in her ears.

"The visions are continuing even though I'm awake. I can't get away from them! They even followed me into the bathroom! They won't leave me alone. God! I wish I knew how to stop them." Diana raked her hair back with outstretched fingers. She gulped, then continued. "The girl is knocked out on drugs or something. I think he's doped her up, but she's still alive. He's taken her back to that same apartment where I was when I felt like I was the little boy. The apartment where he was when he was beating that other woman, the one from the waiting room, your other client. I started shaking the minute I saw it again. But the woman and the kid are gone now. They got away, didn't they?"

Zoe said nothing but nodded slightly. *The girls are okay. Mrs. Randall saw them in the library as usual. They're safe at school. Just breathe slowly and deeply. Breathe from the diaphragm. Keep calm. Don't let Diana's panic get to you. Focus on Diana. You're afraid he's got one of the kids but you have no real evidence for that. Focus on Diana. Stay with her.*

"Anyway, he's taken off the girl's clothes. He's stripped her naked. It's cold in the apartment and she has goose bumps. God, I see everything, or more like I feel everything. He's not the same as before, though. Before he was more, like, mean than crazy, but now he's totally nuts, like off his rocker! He lights all the candles around her. Now he's taking all of his clothes off, too. He's picking her up. She's really just a kid, about fifteen or so, maybe sixteen. He's so disgusting what he's thinking. She's lucky he's drugged her because at least she's still knocked out. He's putting her in a homemade coffin. Now he's leaving to go into the kitchen. He's got those big yellow plastic garbage can ties with the zig-zag edges. He's turning her over, putting her face down in the coffin. He's tying her wrists together behind her back with the plastic things. He pulls them so tight that he hurts her. Her face is smashed up against the bare wood of the coffin. She's starting to rouse. She's moaning. She doesn't know where she is. And you know what's weird?"

"What?" Zoe asked, afraid to hear the answer.

"You know how you like butterflies and your office is all decorated with butterflies?"

"Yes," Zoe said, almost inaudibly.

"How I said I felt like she was you, somehow, but not you?"

"Yes."

"And you know how I said I felt the danger all around you?"

"Yes." *Where is she going with this?*

"Well, this girl has a butterfly tattoo on her shoulder. Isn't that weird? Like maybe she is symbolically you in my unconscious or something."

Zoe felt this information nauseating her stomach even before it registered in her mind. Terror swirled around her, gradually engulfing her, creeping up her skin like fetid water rising in a flood, leaving only gasps of air in tiny pockets near the ceiling. *Please, God, no! It can't be Rebecca! It can't be my Rebecca!* "Diana, listen to me. I am taking what you are saying very seriously. The girl you are describing could be my daughter. I feel like I have to go and check on her now, to make sure she's safe. I'm so sorry but we're going to have to end the session. I'll call you later."

"Oh, Jesus wept! Your daughter! That's okay. Just hurry! Maybe it hasn't happened yet! Maybe there's still time!"

Zoe grabbed her file on Tina Ormond, flung on her coat and was flying out to the car before Diana even stood up. Diana sobbed, exhausted and stunned until the gripping forced her to run for the bathroom again. Only after she came out of the bathroom did she realize that she still had Zoe's pillow clutched tightly in her arms. She started to return it to the receptionist at the front desk, but she quickly changed her mind. Using her index finger, she slowly traced the outline of the needlepoint butterfly that graced the pillow. *This pillow will be safer with me. I'll see Zoe again soon and I can give it back to her then. I wouldn't want anything bad to happen to it.*

CHAPTER 30

Rebecca, Leah and Joe

"*B*ecca, who do you think is more stricter, Mom or Dad?" Leah asked as they waited in front of The Ashcroft School for Zoe to pick them up. They sat on the concrete retaining wall by the big weeping willow tree where all the kids waited for their parents to come and get them after work.

"More strict, not more stricter," Rebecca said authoritatively.

"Whatever," Leah said impatiently, unlacing and re-lacing her leather shoes. Every few minutes another car had arrived and groups of kids filed into cars, minivans and SUV's, until Rebecca and Leah were the last ones there.

Rebecca was writing "Mr. and Mrs. Stephen Jenkins," and practicing the signature "Rebecca Jenkins" in her notebook, dotting the "i" with a little heart. She carefully drew feathers on the arrow that pierced a large heart, decorating the initials R.W. & S.J. with elaborate swirls and flourishes. "I don't know. That's really a tough question. They're strict in different ways."

"Well, like how?" Leah insisted.

"Oh, I don't know. I think Mom is stricter about us fighting and about homework and about writing thank you notes to Bubbe and Zayde and stuff like that. And Mom gets madder at us if she has to come in looking for us and we're not right out front waiting for her after school."

"Dad gets pretty mad about that, too," Leah said.

"Yeah, but Dad doesn't go on the warpath about it like Mom does. And if Mom says she's going to punish us for something if we do it again, then she always does, but Dad sometimes lets us off the hook, especially if we beg long enough."

"If YOU beg long enough, you mean. You have Daddy wrapped around your little finger."

"I do not!" Rebecca retorted.

"Oh, yes you do. What stuff do you think Daddy is more strict about?" Leah asked, as she finished tying her shoes and began applying lip gloss.

"I think he's more strict about stuff like safety rules and wearing hats. If he thinks we might get hurt he won't let us do something no matter what, but sometimes you can reason with Mom about stuff like that if you use good enough arguments. Leah, you're putting on too much of that stuff! You're going to use it all up!"

"Okay," Leah said, carefully returning the cap to the sticky pink lip gloss. "What is up with Dad about the hat thing? He's obsessed."

"Don't ask me. All I know is that he starts talking about how much of your body heat you can lose through the top of your head and going on some long, boring scientific explanation about it," Rebecca said, "Like we care!"

"Mom wants us to wear our hats too, but you can reason with her, at least, and say, 'Mom, I can't wear this hat it's giving me 'hat hair.'"

"Yeah, Mom gets that you have to wear what the other kids wear and Dad is kind of clueless about stuff like that. I don't think he even remembers being a teenager."

"I don't think he ever WAS a teenager," Leah said, giggling.

"Yeah, but Dad remembers being a kid more than Mom, because Dad will go sledding with us in the winter and stuff like that and Mom says she will, but she's always too busy." Rebecca paused, looked worried and uneasy, and then asked, "Leah, who is that man in the red truck?"

"What man?" Leah asked, looking around and noticing Mrs. Randall, the school secretary, holding the telephone and smiling at her out the office window. A small number of school staff remained at Ashcroft until six in order to supervise the children until their parents could pick them up after work.

"Over there," Rebecca pointed to a truck parked beside some pine trees at the far end of the circular driveway in front of the school.

"I don't know, he must be one of the other parents waiting for his kids. I've seen him here a lot lately."

"So have I, but I've never seen his kids get in the car. Whose Dad is he, anyway?"

"How should I know?"

"I keep feeling like he's looking at me," Rebecca said, eyeing the truck suspiciously.

"'Becca, you keep feeling like everybody's looking at you. You're so conceited." Leah said.

"No, really, Leah, he's scaring me," Rebecca said, brows furrowed.

Leah gasped. "Oh, my God!"

"What? What?" Rebecca asked urgently, nervously eyeing the man in the red truck.

"I left my book bag in the library and it's about to close!"

"Don't do that!" Rebecca said.

"Do what?" Leah asked, raising both her shoulders and turning the palms of her hand upwards.

"Don't gasp like that! You scared me to death!" Rebecca said, exhaling loudly and placing her hand on her chest.

"I have to go get my bookbag! Watch my stuff, I'll be right back," Leah said, running up the steps two at a time.

"Wait a minute!" Rebecca said, her cool sophistication quickly dissolving in the face of her fears. "Don't leave me alone!"

"I'll be back in one minute," Leah called out from the top of the stairs. "Just chill, 'Becca! Mom's going to be here any second! Stay there or she'll be mad we're not out front waiting."

"Wait a minute!" Rebecca wailed as Leah disappeared into the library.

The man in the red truck put on sunglasses and pulled down the brim of his greasy green baseball cap. He drove up, got out of the truck, surveyed the surroundings and began to close in on Rebecca from behind. Rebecca bit her fingernails as she kept a vigil waiting for Leah to re-appear, facing back towards the library. Joe clamped a handkerchief full of chloroform over Rebecca's nose and mouth, muffling her screams. Rebecca wildly tried to kick him as he pulled her into the truck's cab, roughly pushing her down and out of view. By the time Leah returned from the library, Rebecca was gone and the red truck was no where to be seen. One minute was all it took.

CHAPTER 31

Zoe and Leah

Zoe screeched out of her office parking lot, yanking her seat belt and latching it as she went. She frantically reached for the cell phone to call the school again.

"Mrs. Randall? This is Zoe Wentworth again. Are the children okay?"

"Why, yes, Mrs. Wentworth. Are you sure you're okay?" Mrs. Randall asked with what Zoe thought was a rather haughty voice.

"Are they still in the library?"

"No, I'm looking at them right now out the front window. They're sitting on the wall."

"Can you see both of them?"

"Yes, is there something wrong?"

"Yes. I have reason to believe that somebody is trying to kidnap them!"

"What? Your voice is breaking up. I think I'm losing you."

Zoe cursed the cell phone and the power lines she was driving by outside that seemed to disrupt the connection. She called back but the line was busy. On the third attempt, she finally got through. "Mrs. Randall? My kids, are my kids all right? I'm afraid someone is trying to kidnap them."

"Oh, my goodness! Well, I believe they're right out front." Mrs. Randall was startled to look back where the children had been just a moment ago only to see no one at all. "Wait. I can't see them now. Let me go check."

Leah came running up the steps towards the office, almost colliding with Mrs. Randall as she headed outside.

"Your mother has been calling and asking for you. Where is your sister?"

"I don't know. She was right on the wall where we always sit just a minute ago."

Mrs. Randall took charge like commander-in-chief. "Leah, please come into the office and stay right with me. Your mother wants you to wait inside."

"My mother wants us to wait inside?" Leah asked in disbelief.

"Yes."

"Are you sure?"

"Yes." Mrs. Randall hurried back to the phone. "Mrs. Wentworth? I don't see Rebecca yet but I've found Leah. She's with me. I'll have everyone left on campus search for Rebecca."

"Thank you. I'm less than half a mile from the school now. I'll be right there." Zoe felt an eerie calm, as if she were suspended in the eye of a hurricane. She gripped the cell phone again and called 911. They forwarded the call to the Marlborough Police Department. Zoe's throat tightened, gripping her vocal cords and straining her speech, but she managed to speak with some difficulty. "My name is Zoe Wentworth. My daughter is missing from the Ashcroft School. I have reason to believe that she has been kidnapped, and I think I know who might have her. I believe he intends to hurt her or kill her. He's been stalking her. The man's name is Joseph Ormond and he lives at 3154 Lincoln Street, Apartment 6-C. He's taken her there. Did you get that address? Please hurry! It's a matter of life and death. Please! There may be no time left!"

"We'll send a car to that address right away, Ma'am. How old is your daughter?"

"Sixteen."

"Are you at home now?"

"No, I'm calling you from my car phone," Zoe said, pulling into the Ashcroft parking lot.

"Can you come into the station to file a missing person's report? The more information we have the better chance we have of finding your daughter."

"Okay! I'll be right there. I'm on my way."

Zoe arrived at the Ashcroft office to find Leah in tears. "Mommy, Rebecca's lost. Everybody who's still here has been searching for her and we can't find her anywhere. She said a man in a red truck was looking at her, but I thought he was just one of the other kids' dads. It's all my fault! I left her alone and she was scared!"

"We're going to go to the police. We can talk on the way there."

"We'll keep looking here, Mrs. Wentworth," Mrs. Randall called out as they turned to leave. "I've paged the headmaster and we'll keep looking."

Zoe and Leah jumped into the car and Zoe dialed Daniel's phone number at work. "Damned voice mail!" Zoe said, exasperated that Dan hadn't answered the phone. She spoke after the beep, "Daniel, I think Rebecca's been kidnapped from school. I'm headed for the Marlborough Police Department. When you get this message come to the police station on Route 85."

Zoe still felt anesthetized, willing herself not to review what Diana had described, unable to take in any envisioned scene that could possibly include Rebecca in a makeshift coffin. *This is going to be bad once it hits me.* Leah's wails were getting louder. "Becca's gone and it's all my fault! Why did I leave her alone?"

"Sweetheart, this is NOT your fault. You had no way of knowing this was going to happen."

"But Mommy, you don't understand!" Leah said, snuffling and sobbing. "I always wished Rebecca would just go away and now she's gone. It really is my fault!" Leah's cries were intensifying and she was covering her face with her hands.

"Honey, do you remember what Mr. Rogers used to say on TV about exactly this kind of feeling?"

"Mr. Rogers! Of course I don't remember Mr. Rogers! How old do you think I am?" Leah glared at her mother angrily through tear drenched eyes.

"He used to say 'angry mad wishes don't make things come true.' No matter what happens it won't be because you had angry wishes. We all have angry wishes, especially about our siblings, and that's O.K."

"Mom, are you crazy? Somebody just kidnapped Rebecca and you're trying to tell me 'It's a beautiful day in the neighborhood!' or something! Mom! Don't you understand? Rebecca's gone! What's wrong with you! You're not even crying!"

"I think I'm just too terrified to cry," Zoe said, her trembling hands gripping the steering wheel as they pulled up in front of the police station. Time seemed suspended, as Zoe got out of the car and rushed into the police station. Zoe answered question after question feeling like she wasn't really there, like nothing that was happening was real. Had there been a quarrel at home? Was there a boyfriend involved? Did Rebecca use drugs or alcohol? Would Rebecca have had some reason to run away? What was the connection between the alleged perpetrator and the family? How had Zoe obtained the information that she shared? Zoe was reluctant to let the officers know that she had gotten her information from a psychic, afraid that this would damage her credibility. She pulled her social work license out of her wallet and showed it to the officer, making sure to use language that would establish her as a professional.

Meanwhile, another officer interviewed Leah, while still another was on the phone to Ashcroft, gathering information from Mrs.

Randall. The computer was checked, looking for prior arrests for Joseph Ormand. There were several calls from a neighbor in an adjoining apartment about domestic disturbances which had not resulted in any arrests because both parties had denied that there was any problem when the police had gotten there. Daniel arrived looking bewildered and stunned as he was told about his daughter being abducted. Soon he was part of the buzz in the hive, answering questions about Rebecca. National missing persons organizations were contacted and up-dated.

Zoe felt frozen, felt vacant, felt nothing at all, while Leah cried softly. Dan approached Zoe and he hugged her tightly. "I'm so scared," he said, tears silently running down his face. Deep sobs finally wracked Zoe as Daniel's tears melted the feelings that were frozen inside of her. "We'll get her back, honey," Daniel said. "We have to get her back." Leah approached her parents and Daniel, Zoe and Leah all hugged, clinging together and crying. The remnants of the fractured family embraced the missing space where Rebecca would have been.

CHAPTER 32

Missing!

*J*oe held a can of Coke laced with Rohypnol to Rebecca's mouth demanding that she drink it. She eyed it suspiciously and clenched her mouth closed. "I said drink it, or I'll cut your throat open and pour it down the bloody hole!" Joe commanded. Rebecca's hands were trembling, so Joe pushed her head back and forced the liquid down her. "Now take all of your clothes off and get in the coffin, face down!"

"No, please!" Rebecca cried.

"I said take them all off or I'll rip them off!" he roared.

Color rose to Rebecca's face as she took off all of her clothes, trying to turn away before Joe grabbed her, forcing her to face him. Joe smiled as he noticed her nipples stiffen in the chilly room.

"How old are you?"

"Sixteen."

"Nice set of knockers, Sweet Sixteen. Now get in the box!"

"No, please," Rebecca cried.

"No, please," Joe mimicked in a high-pitched voice. "Now get in the Goddamned box or I'll fill it up with pieces of you!" Joe bellowed.

"What are you going to do?" Rebecca whimpered.

"We're going to have a religious ceremony, so say your prayers."

Joe approached the coffin, looming above Rebecca, and tied her hands together behind her back. She was beginning to become drowsy from the drug. *And now it is time to prepare the sacrifice.* Joe pulled a large folded hunting knife out of his pocket, pressed the button to extend the blade, and smiled. He was startled by the sound of the doorbell buzzing. He looked out the peephole and saw a cop. *No one can touch me. I am invincible.* He looked at the statue of the Madonna with fixed, glassy eyes. *Holy Mother, avenge my son, as your Son, too, has been avenged.* He closed the knife blade, put it back in his pocket, cracked open the door and peered out suspiciously.

"Are you Joseph Ormond?" the cop wanted to know.

"Yeah. What of it?" Joe asked, scratching the hair on his exposed chest. *He cannot touch me. I am cleansed by the blood of the Lamb.*

"Marlborough Police Department. Officer O'Brien, here. Do you mind if I come in and ask you a few questions?"

"Well, usually I wouldn't mind, Officer," Joe said through a narrowly opened crack, "but my wife and child are very sick in the other room." *The sacrifice is moaning. Writhe in agony. Soon you shall be forever silent.* "That must be my wife now. I'm very sorry, officer, but I'm afraid that I have to go."

"Are those candles I smell in there?" the officer asked, trying to peer inside, but Joe shut the door abruptly.

Joe felt a surge of omnipotence. *I am powerful, rising, strong and magnificent! I rise up, throbbing, pulsating with rhythmic blood.* Joe looked out the window to see the officer getting back in his car and driving away. *Sweet Jesus, the firstborn girl child is mine! 'An eye for an eye and a tooth for a tooth.' As the first born son was taken, so shall the firstborn daughter be taken. First I must anoint myself in preparation.*

Officer O'Brien got in the squad car, drove it a block away and then radioed in to the station. "This Ormond character seemed very nervous. I smell a perp. He refused to let me into the apartment. I couldn't see much from the door, but I did hear a female moaning, and I smelled candles burning, or incense or something."

"Did you get a good look inside?"

"No, I couldn't see anybody. He said his wife was sick, and I could hear a female moaning in the other room, but I couldn't see anything."

"Did you see a red GMC truck in the vicinity?"

"Lemme check it out." O'Brien walked across the street from the parking lot of the apartment, being careful to stay out of view.

"Yeah, there's a red GMC truck in the parking lot in the space marked Apartment 6-C. I believe that's Ormond's apartment."

"O.K. Hang on."

Sergeant Le Blanc and Lieutenant Rice conferred. Both found it oddly suspicious that the mother was neither hysterical nor crying until after her husband got there. Still, the child could not be located at school despite a more thorough search of the school grounds conducted by all of the students and coaches who stayed for after school sports. Zoe Wentworth was a licensed professional who had a connection to the perpetrator, his wife and his child. If Mrs. Wentworth had taken the little boy and his mom out of state, as her records indicated, how could his wife be moaning in the other room? And why would Mr. Ormond refuse to open the door if he had nothing to hide? Despite some minor reservations, they issued a search warrant.

"O'Brien," Le Blanc said. "We're sending you back-ups. Stay where you are. We're going in with the team."

Christ! My heart feels like a jackhammer! That was a close call. Fucking cops! How dare they interrupt the ceremony? He took out his hunting knife and extended the blade just above Rebecca's exposed back. He pulled it up high enough to plunge it in deeply. The voices were getting louder now. *Do not defile the sacrifice until you anoint yourself with blood!* Joe took the knife and jammed it into his own leg, roaring in pain as he twisted and dug the blade through his sinewy flesh. He watched his leg, transfixed as he saw his blood spurting out with every heartbeat. He placed his hand in the still-warm blood, bringing it to his lips to taste it. He smeared it all over his chest, swabbing himself as he listened to a staccato of his own pounding heartbeats syncopated with dripping blood. He felt his penis stiffen as he looked at Rebecca's smooth and rounded creamy white flesh, remembering the frenzied ecstasy of whipping Tina. *Before this little bitch is sacrificed, she's getting it in the ass.*

Boom! The front door splintered into the apartment, shattering the scene as swarms of uniformed police arrived. They were all unprepared for the ghastly scene in front of them. The victim was a naked teenaged girl tied at the wrists with yellow plastic straps, lying face down in a plain pine coffin. It was placed on a large table in the middle of the living room. The room was darkened and the draperies were closed, but the coffin, illuminated by flickering votive candles, revealed a homemade altar with pictures of a dark-haired little boy, an old woman, and a statue of the Virgin Mary.

The smell of the candles didn't quite mask the smell of rotting food mixed with dirty laundry and stale cigarette smoke. The perpetrator was leaning over the coffin with a dripping, bloody knife raised above the girl. Two officers grabbed the knife and locked handcuffs onto Joe's blood-slippery hands.

"Rebecca? Are you Rebecca Wentworth?" one of the cops asked, noticing that her long brown hair was matted and drenched with blood.

"Uh, huh," Rebecca said, barely audibly.

The EMT's moved with startling speed as they prepared to take her to the UMass Marlborough Hospital, just a few blocks away. As the EMT's quickly covered Rebecca's exposed body and secured her to the stretcher, she lifted her head, crying, "Mom? I want my mom!"

"We're taking you to the hospital now, honey, and you can see your mom there," one of the EMT's told her, patting her arm reassuringly as they left.

"What about my son! They kidnapped my son! I'm the victim here!" Joe roared.

"Sit down and shut the fuck up, you sick bastard!" Officer O'Brien said, shoving him onto a chair. One of the EMT's stayed a few steps behind to firmly bind a tourniquet on Joe's still bleeding leg, until a second ambulance could be called.

Joe was sobbing. "Joey! Joey! My son!"

O'Brien called in to the station and asked for Lieutenant Rice. "We have the Wentworth kid and she's alive. The perp is in custody."

Lieutenant Rice broke into a broad smile as he turned to face the Wentworth family. "We've got your daughter and she's still alive!"

CHAPTER 33

The Wentworths at the Hospital

Zoe felt like she was holding her breath all of the way to the hospital. She asked Daniel to stop the car and she jumped out in front of the emergency room entrance, telling Daniel to come and meet her after he parked the car. *Please, God. Please be okay.* She identified herself as Rebecca's mother to the triage nurse who told her to wait and the doctor would be out to speak with her shortly. *Shemah, Yisrael, Adonai Elohenu, Adonai Echad. Hear O Israel, the Lord is our God, the Lord is One.* Silently, she began reciting Psalm 121 of King David, which she had memorized as a child.

> *I lift my eyes to the mountains,*
> *What is the source of my help?*
> *My help comes from Adonai,*
> *Maker of heaven and earth.*
> *God will not let your foot give way;*
> *Your Protector will not slumber.*
> *See, the Protector of Israel*
> *neither slumbers nor sleeps.*

God is your protection at your right hand.
The sun will not strike you by day,
nor the moon by night.
God will guard you from all harm.
God will guard your soul,
Your going and coming,
Now and forever. Amen.

Daniel and Leah rushed in and Zoe told them she hadn't heard anything yet, but that the doctor would be coming out any minute. Leah sat between her parents with her hands on both of their shoulders. Zoe bit her trembling lips, Daniel bit his fingernails and Leah cried softly. A young woman came out and identified herself as Dr. Covey. "Your daughter has been drugged. When she first came in she was covered with blood and we naturally worked to identify the source of the bleeding. We were unable to do that which means that we see no sign of any external or puncture wounds. It appears that the man who kidnapped her cut himself, according to information we received from the EMT's who were on the scene, and it could be his blood which was covering her."

"Is she hurt? Is she going to be okay?" Zoe asked.

"Naturally, we have also been checking for internal injuries. We are doing a toxicology screen to determine what drugs are in her system, and we'll be better able to tell you that after we get the results," Dr. Covey said.

"Was she, did he, has she been violated?" Daniel sputtered.

"I'm sorry we don't have all the answers yet," Dr. Covey said gently.

"Did the kidnapper hurt my sister?" Leah asked, crying.

"We're doing everything we can to take care of your sister," Dr. Covey said.

"Is she conscious?" Zoe asked.

"Yes, but she is very disoriented and sleepy. She is beginning to wake up briefly, and she is responding to her name."

"How soon can we see her?" Zoe asked.

"She's in the process of being admitted. The perpetrator was in the E. R. yelling obscenities, so we got her out of there as soon as we could. As soon as she's cleaned up and settled in her room you can see her."

"Thank you. Thank you so much," Zoe said, exhaling audibly.

She sobbed, covering her face with the palms of her still-trembling hands. Daniel sat with his arm around Leah, stroking her hair to comfort her as she wept, while Zoe pulled out her cell phone to call her parents.

"Mama? Everybody is okay now, but Rebecca was kidnapped from school!" Zoe's voice choked, clutched and seized into loud gasping wails. "My heart has been in my throat, Mama. I thought we were going to lose our baby. I couldn't even cry, I couldn't breathe, I couldn't believe it was really happening." Zoe continued crying as she listened to her mother's response, before she resumed her side of the conversation. "I felt dazed. I felt like everything was happening to somebody else, like it was all just a scene from a horror movie! No, no. He doped her up but we think she's going to be okay. I have to go now because the nurse is here to talk to us. I'll call you back just as soon as I can. Yes, I promise. I promise. Gotta go now and talk to the doctor. Bye, Mama."

The nurse guided the family members down the long hospital corridor that reflected every fluorescent light in the glossy, freshly-polished floor. Zoe rushed to her daughter's bedside.

"Rebecca?" Zoe asked, but Rebecca only groaned.

"She's still very groggy from the drugs. I think she may have to sleep it off for a while," the nurse said.

Zoe took Rebecca's hand and held it tightly, feeling its warmth, reassuring herself that Rebecca was really alive. Daniel placed his hand on top of Zoe's. They waited until Rebecca began to stir.

"'Becca. 'Becca, Sweetheart, it's Mom and Dad. We're here."

"Mom? Dad?" Rebecca asked. "Mommy!" Rebecca said, reaching up into her mother's arms. "I thought that lunatic was going to kill me! He made me get in a coffin." Rebecca said, wailing, choked with tears. "He forced me to take off all my clothes. It was so horrible! I was so scared!"

"Did he rrr, did he er, molest, uh, did he do anything sexual to you?" Daniel asked.

"No! I think he was going to but the police got there in time. He was making these lewd comments. That would have been so disgusting! I don't remember everything, but I don't think so."

"'Becca, I'm so sorry I left you alone! You were right. I guess that guy was looking at you." Leah's crying got louder. "It was my fault because I left you alone."

"That's okay, Leah. It's not your fault. Mom, I just want to go home. When can I go home?"

"They want to keep you at least overnight."

"Why?"

"They need to keep you under observation to make sure you're okay because you were drugged and they still don't have all the test results back."

"Oh my God, I was so terrified. I have never been so scared in my whole life! He had these crazy eyes. It was so hideous. Daddy!" Rebecca reached up for her father and then rocked back and forth in his arms. "Don't let me go, Daddy. Keep holding me," Rebecca whispered.

"It's okay, honey. It's okay. You're safe now. Everything is going to be okay."

"But he's here! I heard him yelling in the E.R. He's still here!" Rebecca said, with panic rising in her voice.

"Not anymore, honey. The police have taken him to jail now. You've been asleep for a while. He's not here anymore," Zoe said.

"Is he really gone?" Rebecca asked the nurse who had just entered the room in order to check Rebecca's vital signs again.

"Oh, he's long gone," the nurse said. "I saw the police take him away in handcuffs myself. Just rest easy now."

"How are you feeling, honey?" Zoe asked.

"I feel better. I don't think he hurt me. I can't remember everything, but nothing hurts and I don't see any cuts or bruises on my body. I thought he was going to kill me!"

"That must have been so terrifying," Zoe exclaimed.

"Oh my God, 'Becca! We were so scared! No one could find you. You just disappeared. We didn't know where you went," Leah said.

"He grabbed me from behind and I didn't know what happened. He shoved me down on the floor in the front seat of his truck. I didn't know where he was going to take me or what he was going to do. I was petrified! Then he takes me to this smelly gross apartment with this big coffin right in the middle of the room. He had these creepy little candles all around it. I thought, 'Oh my God, what a psycho! He's going to kill me and bury me in that coffin.' Rebecca started crying again and Zoe held her tightly. The phone rang and Leah answered it. "It's for you, Becca. It's Stephen."

"Stephen?" Rebecca grabbed the phone, her tears returning as she told Stephen about the ordeal, her voice in hushed tones. "This is on the news?" Rebecca suddenly asked, her voice rising in dismay. "How embarrassing!"

"Let's turn on the TV!" Leah said.

"No," Daniel said. "Your sister has been through enough as it is."

Leah sidled up to Dan and said, "Dad, I'm really getting hungry and I have a lot of homework left to do. When can we go home?"

Dan looked at Zoe, who said, "How do you feel about me taking her home?"

"I'd be okay with it, if Rebecca is okay with it."

"Excuse me, Rebecca," Zoe said, interrupting the telephone conversation. "Are you okay with Dad taking Leah home now?"

"Will you stay here with me, Mom?"

"Yes. I'll be here with you."

"Okay. But I wish I could go home, too."

Daniel hugged Rebecca and kissed her on the cheek. "It's so good to know you're safe."

Leah went up to her sister and hugged her goodbye. "I'm glad the kidnapper didn't kill you. If you want the front seat this week you can have it."

"Thanks, Lee Lee."

"I'll call you as soon as I hear anything more," Zoe said to Dan as they left. "Take care."

"Mom, would you mind taking a little walk or something? I'd kind of like a little privacy so I can talk to Stephen," Rebecca asked.

"Sure, honey," Zoe said, fighting the instinct not to let Rebecca out of her sight. Zoe walked down the hall looking at room after room of sick and injured patients, thinking about how lucky she was that they found Rebecca in time. She called her mother on her cell phone. "Mama, it's me. We talked to the doctors and we saw her. She looks good. Better than I expected. She didn't have any wounds on her body but they're checking for internal injuries. She doesn't seem to be in any pain, but naturally she is quite shaken. He gave her some kind of drugs or something. Tell Papa she's going to be okay. She'll pull through. Yeah, I'm O.K. Yes, I'll call you again as soon as we know anything more, and I'll have Rebecca call you so you can hear her voice." Zoe remembered that she needed to call Diana too, so she dialed the number after taking a quick peek to see Rebecca from the hallway.

"Hullo?"

"Diana, this is Zoe. I'm sorry I had to rush out of the session like that, but I don't know how to thank you enough. Your vision was completely accurate in every detail. Because you told it to me the police were able to rescue my daughter in time."

"Wow! She's okay? I've been watching it on the news and all they said is that they took her to the hospital. But she's okay?"

"Yes. She's scared and shaken, but she's going to be okay."

"I'm so relieved to hear that. I've been so scared."

"Because you shared your vision with me, you saved my daughter's life."

"Wow!" Diana said, pausing to take in the enormity of that. "So it really did happen just like it was in the dream?"

"Yes. It was eerie to learn how accurate your dream was, down to the smallest detail. We can talk about it some more at our next session."

"When do I see you again, at my regular appointment time next week?"

"Yes. I reserve that time for you."

"Okay, I'll see you then. Thank you."

"And thank you, Diana. Thank you for your extraordinary and powerful gift."

CHAPTER 34

Zoe and Jessica at the Wayside Inn

Zoe's boots crunched through the thin layer of ice that frosted the snow leading up to the heavy black front door of the Wayside Inn in Sudbury. The historic red inn, dating back to 1697, was the setting for *Tales of a Wayside Inn*, Longfellow's American version of Chaucer's *Canterbury Tales*. It looked particularly lovely in contrast to the white snow surrounding it, especially when decorated for Christmas with a wreath and candle adorning each window. Zoe searched the lobby area, saw no sign of Jessica but decided to ask for a table anyway. Festive arrangements of fruits on the fireplace mantle and ribbon decorated garlands adorned the dining room. Golden glass ornaments hung from each chandelier, reflecting the lights from the electric candles.

Jessica arrived a few minutes late, uncharacteristically, and put down the Chanukah gift she had brought for Zoe. They ordered their food from a pleasantly plump woman dressed in colonial garb, then Zoe took a small Christmas gift for Jessica out of a bag and put it on the table.

"How are you holding up, Zoe?" Jessica asked, patting the top of Zoe's hand as it rested on the table.

"I'm hanging in there, I guess. It's been hard for all of us. Half of the time I feel terrified, thinking about how close we came to having our secure lives destroyed in moments. The other half of the time I feel so blessed because we got Rebecca back," Zoe said, tears moistening her eyes.

"It's been a difficult year for you, hasn't it?"

Zoe looked deeply and gratefully into the hazel eyes of her friend, noting the beauty of the multicolored specks in her iris. "Yes, it has been. Usually it's just the daily hassles of being a working mom and the struggles inherent in relationships, but nothing prepared me for the bombshell of a kidnapping detonating in our lives. I remember how I felt when Rebecca was gone, terrified for her. I can't imagine what it must be like for mothers who are not so lucky. I can't even fathom feeling what I felt for months or years. It was absolutely unbearable for one afternoon and evening." Zoe swallowed hard, and took a sip of water to bathe her dry mouth.

"When you called me that night, I remember thinking that I have never heard such anguish in your voice, and that was <u>after</u> you knew she was safe."

"Throughout the whole ordeal I wouldn't even allow myself to feel it. I just went numb. It was like emotionally, I was under general anesthesia, or something," Zoe said, in hushed tones as the waitress put salads in front of them and brought them a basket of warm whole wheat rolls and cornbread stone ground at the gristmill across the street.

"You must have been frantic," Jessica said, stabbing her salad with her fork.

"We've all been feeling so fragile after what has happened, like the tidy mythology of our safety and protection has been ruptured. But our love for each other and our sense of resiliency feels stronger than ever. Naturally, it's Rebecca I've been most worried about. When we were lighting the Chanukah candles last week Rebecca started to cry, sobbing because the smell of the candles brought her back to that terrible day."

"Oh, that must have been so hard for her. Smells are so evocative of memories."

"Yes, and it hasn't been that long. But I told her not to forget that we were celebrating miracles as we were lighting the candles on the menorah, the most important one being her survival. Our people have been celebrating our survival for centuries, despite what evil ones have done to try to destroy us." The waitress returned with their lunch entrees, briefly suspending conversation while the plates were placed on the table.

Jessica carefully separated her carrots, mashed potatoes and chicken so that nothing was touching on her plate. "When something like this happens, I think it sharpens the focus of what is really most important in life."

"That's so true. I've been thinking about my life a lot lately. I realize that both as a mother and as a therapist I am helping other people grow. I never stop feeling privileged to be a witness to that metamorphosis."

"When I hear the word metamorphosis it reminds me of how much you love butterflies."

"Yes, and that's why I love them. Even though their change process is scientific and predictable, it never stops feeling like a miracle. It's like with my psychic client, she has really blossomed ever since the successful rescue she enabled. She has felt validated by what has happened, instead of being so afraid."

Jessica took a big gulp of water while she pondered this. "You know, I still feel so uncomfortable when you call your client 'psychic.' It's not even like I disagree with you, it's more like I have no idea what that really means. I just don't get it. How do you explain it?"

"I explain it as a gift As a therapist my job is to help Diana to accept herself as she is and to stop being afraid of her own power. But Diana has also brought me a powerful gift and so does every client I work with, though usually not in such a dramatic way. I have felt a Sacred Presence working with me and working through me, but I have always been afraid to claim it, afraid of stepping outside of my professional training. After this case, I feel blessed and privileged to bear witness to my clients' growth. I feel so much more connected to the process of spiritual growth and to measuring my own success with that as the crux of my work."

"You lost me when you got into all this spiritual gobbledygook. See, I think your skills are what's helping your clients. Scientific, research-based, sound clinical skills. You can believe whatever you want, Zoe, but you're a fine clinician and I personally don't think you need any help from God or anyone else." Jessica carefully removed the napkin from her lap smoothing and folding it before neatly putting it back where she had found it.

"Would you ladies like some coffee or dessert?" asked the waitress, noting that they had stopped eating their lunch.

"No thank you, I think we're all set," Jessica said.

"O.K. then, I'll bring you your check."

"Do you want to open your present now or to save it for Christmas?" Zoe asked.

"What would you like me to do?"

"Open it now. I love watching you open the gifts I've gotten you," Zoe said, leaning forward in her chair.

Jessica slowly and carefully took her Swiss army knife out of the pocket in her black wool trousers, and surgically made a small incision dissecting the scotch tape from the wrapping paper.

Zoe laughed. "You remind me of Dan, the way you do that so precisely. Leah always jumps up and runs across the room and rips it open whenever he's opening a gift like that."

"This wrapping paper is so pretty that I didn't want to tear it." Jessica opened the present and began to chuckle when she saw the gift. "This is too funny."

"What?" Zoe asked.

"Open your Chanukah present," Jessica said.

Zoe opened her gift quickly and she also began laughing as soon as she saw it. "What are the chances of this?" she asked. They had both gotten each other identical hand mirrors covered with delicate butterflies in muted tones of blue and purple.

"I really, really love this. I got you this mirror because you love butterflies, but how did you know to get it for me?" Jessica asked.

"I just loved it so much I thought you would love it too. It was in your colors and it looked like something I would see in your office. I guess I just trusted my instincts." Zoe said, smiling broadly.

"So what do we call this one, 'Deja Vu Times Two'?" Jessica asked, picking up her mirror briefly to look at her own reflection.

"That's pretty good. After all, "'Deja Vu All Over Again' has already been done."

"Or how about Deja View?"

"I like that. 'Deja View' it is," Zoe said, satisfied.

0-595-26769-6